D1473701

Seeing Red

Especially for Girls ® Presents

::·HOLLYWOOD·::
WARS

Seeing Red

ILENE COOPER

P U F F I N   B O O K S

PUFFIN BOOKS
Published by the Penguin Group
Penguin Books USA Inc., 375 Hudson Street, New York, New York 10014, U.S.A.
Penguin Books Ltd, 27 Wrights Lane, London W8 5TZ, England
Penguin Books Australia Ltd, Ringwood, Victoria, Australia
Penguin Books Canada Ltd, 10 Alcorn Avenue, Toronto, Ontario, Canada M4V 3B2
Penguin Books (N.Z.) Ltd, 182-190 Wairau Road, Auckland 10, New Zealand

Penguin Books Ltd, Registered Offices: Harmondsworth, Middlesex, England

First published in the United States of America by Puffin Books,
a division of Penguin Books USA Inc., 1993

1 3 5 7 9 10 8 6 4 2

Cooper, Ilene.
Seeing red / Ilene Cooper.
p. cm.—(A Puffin high flyer) (Hollywood wars; #3)
Summary: When the cast of "Sticks and Stones" takes to the road for a publicity tour, the uneas
truce between the two stars is threatened by Jamie's ego and Alison's stage fright.
ISBN 0-14-036157-X
[1. Television programs—Fiction. 2. Actors and actresses—Fiction. 3. Friendship—Fiction.]
I. Title. II. Series: Cooper, Ilene. Hollywood wars; #3.
C7856Se 1993 92-42426 [Fic]—dc20 CIP AC

Printed in the United States of America

High-Flyer TM is a trademark of Puffin Books, a division of Penguin Books USA Inc.

Seeing Red

Chapter 1

"Mom, I don't think stars should help with moving," Jamie called. She flopped down on the couch, kicking a small carton filled with towels out of the way.

Mrs. O'Leary appeared in the kitchen doorway. "You're my daughter first, a star second. Would this be easier if I called the tabloids?" she asked good-naturedly. "I'm sure they'd love to do a feature about television's Wendy helping her mother and little sister get settled in their new home."

Jamie laughed. "No way." She looked down at her once-white blouse and cut-offs, now covered with the grime of moving. "I play a rich girl on *Sticks and Stones.* I couldn't disappoint my fans."

Fans. It seemed strange to even think it. Of course, she had had fans once before. As a kid, she had starred in a comedy series called *The Happydale Girls,* set in an orphanage. That job had lasted until Jamie was nine, when the show ended. It had been a hard readjustment, becoming a nobody and a poor one at that. Now, though, Jamie had a job on the new but very popular television show, *Sticks and Stones*. She played Wendy Stone, whose mother, a wealthy divorcée, is engaged to a garage owner, Joe Stickley. The show had only been on for a couple of weeks, but it was already number one in its time slot, and the network had ordered thirteen more episodes. It looked like *Sticks and Stones* was going to be around for a while, and thank goodness, that meant she was going to be around, too.

Which was why the O'Learys could finally afford to dump their crummy old apartment over the Chinese restaurant. Jamie, her mother, and her four-year-old sister, Elsie, had spent most of the weekend moving into half of a spacious duplex that was large, sunny, and well kept up by their landlady, Mrs. Anderson.

Of course, the apartment couldn't compare with the Westwood home of her co-star, Alison Blake. Jamie sighed enviously. Alison had it all. She was rich, thin, beautiful, and a darn good actress. It still burned Jamie that Alison had gotten the part of Jane Stickley without any experience at all.

Jamie had even tried to get Alison kicked off the show, by coaxing Alison to reinterpret her part without telling the producers. It hadn't worked. Everyone thought the way Alison had changed things was a big improvement.

Since that fiasco, Jamie's feelings about Alison had seesawed back and forth. She was still jealous of Alison. But if she was being honest, Jamie had to admit that Alison had been pretty nice, introducing her to her friends, even getting her out of a sticky situation with her father.

The door to the apartment opened. *Speak of the devil,* she thought, as Mr. O'Leary walked into the room.

Her father's arms were full of grocery bags. "How's it going?" he boomed.

"Okay," Jamie replied, not looking at him. Here was another person she had mixed feelings about. Mr. O'Leary, Jamie's manager during her years on *The Happydale Girls,* had left the family after Jamie's career had stalled, but when this new job came up, Jack O'Leary reappeared, eager to reclaim his role of dad and her manager.

Jamie had been furious. She couldn't get her father to see that his constant attempts to be involved at the studio were embarrassing. As fate would have it, it was Alison who'd had the heart-to-heart talk with Mr. O'Leary that made him see the light.

"I stocked up at Ralph's," Mr. O'Leary said, hefting the bags.

"Well, being a customer sure beats being an employee." Jamie had worked at Ralph's Market before her big break on *Sticks and Stones.* She watched her father head into the kitchen. It was amazing to Jamie that after the way he had left them flat, her mother was ready to welcome him back with open arms.

Jamie had been so angry with her father for so long, it wasn't easy to let go of all those bad feelings. But it seemed like her father wasn't going anytime soon, so Jamie supposed she might as well try to get used to him. At least he now understood that there was no way they were going to be associated professionally. "Thank you Alison," Jamie muttered.

Jamie didn't feel like doing any more unpacking before dinner. Not that she was eating much lately. Jamie had decided that Alison wasn't going to be the only one with a willowy model's figure on the show, so she had put herself on a strict diet. At first it had been a total drag, but now that the weight was slipping off, Jamie didn't notice the hunger nearly as much.

Since dinner was destined to be no big deal, maybe she should take a walk and check out the neighborhood. Jamie stood up and stretched. "I'm going out for a while," she called in the general direction of the kitchen.

Elsie emerged from her bedroom. "Where are you going?" she demanded.

"Just for a walk."

"I want to go too."

Jamie's mouth twitched. No one could get to her like her baby sister. There was no way Elsie could be described as pretty, but her funny face showed more personality than ten actresses Jamie could name.

"We need to make friends in our new neighborhood," Elsie continued seriously.

"It usually takes time to make friends," Jamie cautioned. She didn't want her sister getting her heart broken by some stuck-up kids.

Elsie shook her head. "No, Jamie, just tell them you want to be friends and they will be."

Ah, to have the innocence of a four-year-old. Well, Jamie supposed the least she could do was humor Elsie. "All right, let's go see who lives around here."

Elsie grabbed her best doll, and they headed outside. The

street was pleasantly residential, a far cry from their former down-at-the-heels neighborhood. They strolled for a while, enjoying the summer evening. Elsie pointed out all kinds of things that were new to her: backyards complete with barbecue grills, flowers, even a park with an enticing array of swings, slides, and a merry-go-round.

"Let's go in," Elsie said, tugging at Jamie's hand.

"It's getting late," Jamie warned. "There's not much time for playing."

"Please."

Jamie relented. "Just for a few minutes."

"Okay." Elsie ran into the park, then stopped and looked around as if wondering which great ride to try first. Jamie was about to suggest she push Elsie on the swings when a little Asian girl walked over to her sister. Jamie couldn't hear the conversation except for the word *slide* but within a few seconds, Elsie was following the child.

"I'm going with Jeannie," Elsie called over her shoulder.

Jamie nodded. "I'm right behind you." Apparently, Elsie was right. It was easy to make friends—if you were four.

She made herself comfortable on a bench and watched Elsie and Jeannie go down so many times, she lost count. She knew she should be home studying her lines for tomorrow's run-through or helping put stuff away, but for the first time since she had joined *Sticks and Stones,* Jamie felt utterly and completely relaxed. Being on the show was great, but it was nervewracking. Practically overnight she was back in show business; learning her lines; going to school on the set; dealing with producers, cast members, and crew; and trying to figure how she fit into this whole new world. Add to the mix a back-again father, her don't-eat diet, and a new home. No wonder she sometimes didn't know if she was coming or going.

"A penny for your thoughts."

Startled, Jamie turned at the sound of the male voice. Standing over her was a tall blond boy wearing torn jeans and a Lakers T-shirt. His eyes were blue, but Jamie couldn't quite put her finger on the color. Sky blue, maybe, she decided.

"I guess a penny isn't enough these days. How about a quarter?" he asked with a smile.

"How about a dollar?" Jamie replied pertly.

"Boy, those must be some thoughts." Without an invitation, he sat down next to her.

Jamie shrugged. "Maybe."

The boy stared at her. "Don't I know you from somewhere?"

Not many people had recognized Jamie since the *Sticks and Stones* debut, but Jamie knew from her last go-round on television that before long it would be hard to walk down the street unnoticed. That kind of fame, Jamie knew, could be a mixed blessing. It was fun to watch people's excitement when they realized they were talking to a real live television star, and of course, it was great if they praised her work. But if they followed her around when she was shopping, or came up to her at restaurants, it wasn't so much fun anymore.

Before Jamie could identify herself, the boy snapped his

fingers. "You're on that television show. What's the name of it?"

"*Sticks and Stones*," Jamie murmured.

"That's it."

Jamie waited. Usually, fans got all gushy at this point, but the boy seemed to lose interest in her acting career now that he had identified her. Finally, Jamie decided she had to say something. "So who are you?" she asked. It came out more curtly than she had intended.

"Of course. You wouldn't know me." There was a slightly sarcastic edge to his voice. "David Gable."

David was her favorite name.

"So what are you doing *here*?"

Jamie decided to ignore his tone. "I live around here."

That woke him up. "You're kidding."

"Why should I be kidding?"

"This isn't exactly Beverly Hills, in case you haven't noticed."

"Oh, I've noticed."

"You must feel like you're slumming."

Now Jamie was starting to get mad. "For your information, I just moved here. My family was living in a total dump before I got on *Sticks and Stones*. This seems like heaven to me."

David looked around. "Funny, I haven't noticed."

Jamie got up and called to Elsie. "Time to go."

"Your sister?"

Jamie nodded as Elsie ran up to her. She brushed some dirt off Elsie, who was looking at David curiously.

"I'm Elsie. Who are you?"

"David." He stuck out his hand, and Elsie gave it a solemn shake.

"I made a friend. Her name is Jeannie. Are you Jamie's friend?"

David and Jamie avoided each other's eyes. "I think it's harder to make friends when you get older," David said.

Elsie shook her head. "No it isn't."

David laughed. "Well, maybe your sister and I will get to be friends one day soon."

"Come on, Elsie." Jamie tugged a little on her sister's hand and moved her away. "Mom will start to worry."

"Bye," Elsie called to David. Then she turned to look up at Jamie. "I told you we'd find some friends."

Alison Blake blinked at her mother in surprise. She couldn't believe the bathing suit her mother was holding. "Mom! It's a bikini."

"Oh, I wouldn't say that. It's just a two piece."

Leaning back against her mother's headboard, Alison shook her head. "Face it, Mom, your beautiful new green bathing suit is definitely a teeny bikini."

Mrs. Blake blushed. Like Alison, she had soft red hair and porcelain skin that easily reddened. "So, don't I still have the figure for it?"

"You're the best-looking mom I've ever seen," Alison replied honestly.

Her mother smiled. "That's because I look just like you." She sat down on the bed. "You're sure you don't mind that your father and I are taking this vacation?"

"No, of course not." Saying that came a little easier now

that she'd had to answer that question about a hundred times. When Alison had first heard about the trip, she had felt slightly left out. But as things at work had become busier, Alison had less time to worry about her parents. There were too many things swirling around her own life.

For one thing, her boyfriend, Brad D'amato, was now history. He hadn't been able to handle her sudden change in lifestyle. Alison had also managed to lose her best friend, Dana. In some ways, Alison felt as though she was suspended between two lives. The old one was disappearing, but thinking of herself as an actual television star was so weird, she tried not to think of it at all.

"Hey, what's going on in here, a fashion show?"

Alison looked up to see her father standing in the doorway. Mr. Blake was a lawyer, a very successful one. His career allowed them to live in a beautiful house, take trips, buy almost anything they wanted. Alison knew she was lucky. Even if *Sticks and Stones* went off the air tomorrow, her life would still be pretty nice.

"You know, Clare, we're only going away for ten days," Mr. Blake continued, a smile on his face. He gestured to the clothes strewn across the bed. "There's enough here for an around-the-world cruise."

"Planning for a cruise is no laughing matter," Mrs. Blake countered, but she was laughing a little too.

"Apparently not." He turned to his daughter. "Now, you're going to be all right while we're gone, aren't you, Ali?"

Alison sighed. "Yes, of course." With Estelle, their housekeeper, looking over her shoulder, how could she be anything else? Not that Alison was surprised by her father's question. She knew he still thought of her as shy Ali, his Alison Wonderland.

"I could have stayed by myself."

"You're a little too young for that," Mrs. Blake told Alison, "but you know Estelle won't interfere."

Alison got up. She tried not to let her parents see she was irritated, but as she walked out of the room, she said, "There's nothing to interfere with. I go to work and I come home. Estelle will probably be bored to tears."

Glancing at her watch, Alison wondered what she should do for the next hour or so. She could go over her lines, but she already knew them by heart. It was too early to go to sleep. Maybe she should go downstairs and watch television, but since getting on the show, she couldn't just relax and watch TV like everyone else did. It reminded her too much of what she did all day.

The truth was, Alison didn't really believe she was as good an actress as everyone said she was. At first, she had been delighted with her good reviews, but now that she'd had time to think about it, she was afraid that she was just pulling the wool over everyone's eyes.

Working with professionals, like Ben Epson, who played her father, and Donna Wheeler, her soon-to-be stepmother, Alison was seeing firsthand how real actors knew their craft. After all, unlike Jamie, Alison had no real experience. Lately it seemed like she needed more direction than the rest of the cast. Pretty soon, her inadequacies would start to become apparent to everyone, and then what would she do?

Alison could feel the knot in her stomach tighten, the knot that seemed to be a permanent resident there. That's why she hated watching television. She watched it so much more critically now, and whether it was dramas or comedies, or even the soaps, everyone seemed to be a better actress than she was. They looked better, moved better, and certainly spoke their lines better.

Maybe she should just go read a book. She knew she was no writer, so she couldn't compare herself to an author. But when she got to her lovely bedroom, decorated with flowery English fabrics, Alison didn't pick up her book; she just curled up into a little ball on her bed.

One reason she had wanted so much to get this part in *Sticks and Stones* was so that she could get some of the self-confidence she felt that she was missing. For a while it had worked that way. But now, Alison could feel all the gains she had made dribbling away. She wasn't a real actress. She had just lucked out.

Chapter 2

Jamie walked into the almost empty studio. She looked around at the set, the handsomely decorated living room that belonged to her family, the Stones. With a grin, Jamie flopped down on the velvet couch. It felt wonderful to be on a set. She felt more alive here than she did anywhere else. How had she survived so many years without acting?

She glanced over to the corner of the studio where some of the production people were setting up the usual buffet for the actors and crew. Her smile faded, and Jamie could feel her stomach lurch a little. Doughnuts, muffins, sweet rolls drizzled with icing. They waited on the table, there for the taking. Well, she couldn't have any, she told herself virtuously. Let the others chow down and get fat. She was going to lose weight. Jamie got off the couch and headed for her dressing room. She averted her head as she walked by the buffet. If she started eating she might never stop.

Alison was already in the dressing room, holding this

week's costume up to herself. Turning to Jamie she made a face.

"Boy, could this be duller?"

Jamie shrugged. "You *are* one of the poor Stickleys."

"That doesn't mean I'd always wear a T-shirt and boring jeans. Even people who don't have much money have taste."

"Sure, Alison, but that doesn't mean *we* can afford to go out and buy something that suits our sophisticated tastes."

Alison felt herself blush. Did Jamie have to take every comment she made so personally?

Jamie noticed Alison's embarrassment, but it didn't bother her. Alison had to realize not everyone was rich like she was. Maybe playing Jane Stickley—and having Jamie O'Leary be the voice of her conscience—might help.

"Did you hear about the special meeting Dan's called?" Alison asked, changing the subject.

"No." Jamie frowned. Things were going along great for once. Why a special meeting? Was Dan Greenspan, the show's producer, going to give them bad news, announce a cast change, fire *her*? "What's it about?"

"I haven't a clue. He posted a notice on the bulletin board. He wanted everyone to meet onstage in five minutes."

Jamie walked over to the garment bag that held her own clothes for the show. Even though her costumes also ran to jeans and tops, they always had a special flair that befitted her character, the wealthy Wendy Stone. For this show, Helga, the costumer, had found a gorgeous hand-knit sweater embroidered with tiny roses. The jeans were the expensive designer kind, fashionably faded and torn at the the knees.

"Maybe Dan wants to talk to us about the American Choice Awards," Jamie remarked as she examined the costume she'd wear at the dress rehearsal and taping tomorrow. Some of the cast members were going to give out the statues at the ceremony in which the public voted for their favorite movies, television shows, actors, and actresses.

"You could be right. I've been wondering who Dan's picked to go to New York."

So have I, Jamie thought to herself. *So have I.*

Glancing at her watch, Alison said, "We better get going, Jamie. I'm sure everyone is out there."

"All right, all right." Jamie didn't need Alison rushing her around. Her stomach growled a little. Embarrassed, Jamie wondered if Alison heard the rumble.

By the time the girls arrived, most of the cast members had already gathered. Ben Epson, who played Joe Stickley, stood next to Donna Wheeler, his fiancée on the show, Amanda Stone. With them waited Rodney Janeway, the precocious kid who played Jamie's younger brother, also named Rodney on the show. Only Mike Malone was missing. He had the role of Lucas Stickley, Alison's older brother.

Dan Greenspan, the show's creator and energetic producer, hurried on to the set. "Are we all here?" Frowning, he answered his own question. "No Mike."

"Here I am," Mike responded, ambling over to the group. "Sorry I'm late." He gave Dan the lazy smile that was so popular with the show's female fans—and Alison and Jamie for that matter. But the magnetism was lost on Dan.

"Promptness counts, Mike," Dan said dryly. "But now that we're all here, I've got some very interesting news for all of you."

Interesting, Jamie thought. That didn't sound too bad.

"The network is getting behind *Sticks and Stones* in a big way."

"Well, I should hope so," Ben interjected. "We were number nine in the ratings last week. That's dynamite for a summer replacement."

Dan grinned. "Yeah. Just on the air for a couple of weeks, and already we're in the top ten."

The group spontaneously broke into applause.

"So, you guys are being sent on a major-league publicity tour. We already have one extra show in the can, and *Sticks and Stones* is being preempted next week for a special. So we're going to take next week off, and you'll be sent to different cities to promote the show. I have a schedule here of the talk shows you'll be on. At the end of the week Mike, Jamie, Rodney, and Alison will be presenters on the American Choice Awards in New York.

Jamie didn't even listen to Donna's and Ben's assignments. She could feel her heart beating faster. She was going to be a presenter on a prime-time awards show. This was big stuff.

"Feel up to it?" Dan asked Jamie with a grin.

"I hope so," Jamie said fervently.

Dan started passing out sheets of paper. "Here are your

schedules for the publicity tour. Look them over. If there are any problems, let me know. One of the production assistants will come around later with your airline tickets and your hotel confirmations.''

Jamie barely noticed Dan leaving the set. She was too busy poring over the sheet that he had handed her. At first, it was a little difficult to take it all in. There was a radio interview on Monday morning in Los Angeles. Then it was off to New York. *Yes,* she thought, *there's a modeling session for* Way *magazine! Way* was *the* coolest fashion magazine. Then there were several more interviews, one on a local New York talk show and another one on the *Today* show. The *Today* show!

Alison came up to her. She looked as if she was going to be sick. ''Can I see your schedule sheet?''

''Sure.'' Jamie wondered what was wrong with Alison.

''Ours are the same,'' Alison said, scanning the sheet. ''We're going to New York.''

Jamie wasn't terribly pleased that she and Alison would be joined at the hip for a week, but this trip sounded so great, she decided to tolerate Alison and enjoy herself.

''Oh gosh,'' Alison murmured as she looked over the schedule once more.

''What's wrong?'' Jamie asked.

''The *Today* show.''

''Yeah. So?'' Jamie pretended it was just another interview show.

''I've been watching the *Today* show since I was a little kid.''

"Who hasn't?"

"Doesn't it seem weird to you?" Alison asked. "Being on the *Today* show?"

"Not really. I did lots of talk shows when I was on *The Happydale Girls.*"

"Well, it seems weird to me."

Jamie shrugged. "You can cut your teeth on radio. We've got an interview on Monday."

"That shouldn't be too bad," Alison agreed.

A production assistant came up to Alison and Jamie. "Dan wants to see you in his office."

The girls exchanged glances. "What now?" Jamie muttered.

Dan was on the phone when the girls arrived, but he motioned them to sit down. While they waited, Jamie looked at the modern art hung all over the office. One picture was just a blue canvas with several pink dots strategically placed in three of the four corners. Jamie was sure the picture had cost a lot, but privately, she thought it was lame. Still, it did give her hope that if her acting career fell through again, she could make some money painting.

"I meant to talk to you on the set," Dan said, "but I had to catch this phone call. I realize this trip is very short notice, but when the network decides it wants something . . ." Dan shrugged.

"What about clothes?" Jamie asked timidly. There was no way her personal wardrobe could withstand a trip to the Big Apple.

"Don't worry. We'll outfit you with things from the show. I'm more concerned about getting permission from your parents. I wanted to tell you I'm going to call them now.''

"My mother won't mind," Jamie said quickly.

Alison was silent.

"Do you think your parents will have a problem with you going to New York?'' Dan asked.

''Well, you know they are kind of protective.'' Alison's voice was barely audible. Dan had had enough trouble convincing her parents she should be on the show at all. She wished she could just say, like Jamie, that it was fine for her to go off to New York, but she thought her parents would probably have plenty to say about it.

Jamie picked at her nails, while Dan informed Alison that Cindy Vargas, one of the production people from the show, would be their on-the-road chaperon. She'd also make sure things ran smoothly. Rodney's mother, who watched out for them on the show, would be along to chaperon as well.

''Would either of you like a coach?'' Dan asked.

Jamie frowned. "A coach? What for?''

"To help you bone up for the interviews.''

''I don't think that's necessary, do you?'' Jamie replied.

Dan grinned. ''Not really. You know how to handle yourself. What about you, Alison?''

Alison felt herself blush. Dan probably thought she could use a coach. Well, if Jamie wasn't going to have one, she was darned if she was going to look like some needy novice. Even though she was. ''I'll be fine, too,'' she said, hoping she sounded convincing.

''I think that takes care of everything,'' Dan said. ''You kids better get out there for the run-through.''

Jamie and Alison left for the set. The run-through was a rehearsal done without costumes, but everyone was supposed to know their lines and hit their marks, pieces of tape on the floor that showed the actors where to stand so the director could choose the best camera angles. Today, the run-through was pretty ragged. Maybe it was the news of the publicity tour, but when the rehearsal was over, Kevin Voight, the director, came down from the control booth with a frown on his face.

"I've seen you all do better," he said.

No one said anything, not even Ben and Donna.

Kevin shook his head. "Okay, it happens. I'll give you some notes, and we can try it again tomorrow."

Notes weren't written on pieces of paper. They were the director's spoken comments, telling his cast what needed to be improved about their performances. It took Kevin the better part of an hour to give his notes.

"Wow, I thought we'd never get out of there," Mike muttered as he walked with Alison and Jamie toward their dressing rooms.

"I couldn't keep my mind on the show thinking about the tour," Jamie admitted.

While Mike nodded in agreement, Alison was just glad that everyone had had a bad day. Maybe her own limp performance wasn't so noticeable.

"So where are you starting?" Mike asked.

"On a radio show here in L.A., then on to New York," Jamie informed him.

Mike grinned. "See you in the Big Apple. This might be fun after all."

"You're not on the radio show here?" Alison asked.

"Nope. I start out on *Good Morning, Chicago.*"

"You start with television?" Alison's tone was full of sympathy.

"I'm on television all the time," Mike said with a shrug.

"It's not the same," Alison murmured. Speaking memorized lines was one thing, but answering questions some interviewer was asking out of the blue, well, that was something quite different.

All the way home, Alison wondered how her parents would react to the news of her trip. As nervous as she was already, she certainly hoped that her parents wouldn't put any embarrassing roadblocks in the way. That would be mortifying.

Mr. and Mrs. Blake were in the den when Alison arrived. She noted the worried expressions on their faces.

"I've got to go," Alison burst out before they could say anything.

"We know," Mr. Blake said with a sigh.

"You do? I can?" Alison asked, surprised at his ready agreement.

"When you took the job, your father and I realized there would be more to your career than just acting," her mother told her. "Neither your father nor I are surprised. We've been expecting something like this."

"We're just not very happy about this publicity tour coming up while we're in the middle of a cruise," Mr. Blake said.

"But it works out better this way," Alison replied. "I won't be an extra burden to Estelle because I'll be out of town. And the three of us will be so busy, we won't miss each other so much.''

Her parents exchanged glances. ''I suppose that makes sense,'' her mother said. ''I just can't imagine being out of the country while you're going off on this adventure. Why, Dan said you were going to be on the *Today* show.''

''So we'll tape it.'' Alison knew she was totally skirting the issue. Her parents were worried about being away just when she was facing something important and frightening. But she couldn't help it. She couldn't think about that right now. If she did, every bit of insecurity she had, and that was plenty, might totally overwhelm her.

Mr. Blake pasted a big smile on his face. ''I think Alison is right. We're being silly. She's going on a tour that's a requirement of her professional life. She'll be well-chaperoned, and if her success on *Sticks and Stones* is any indication, the *Today* show will wind up with a few million more viewers tuning in just to see her.''

Alison didn't like to think about the television viewers, much less millions of them, watching her live without a part to hide behind, but she appreciated her father's efforts to make her feel better. ''That's right,'' she said, trying to smile brightly. ''This kind of stuff comes with the territory. I can handle it.''

I hope, she added silently to herself.

Chapter 3

Alison glanced nervously at her watch. She pushed away the cup of coffee that the *On the Scene* production assistant had given her when she had arrived at the radio studio. She already felt pretty wired and the coffee wasn't helping.

Where is Jamie? she wondered. What if she had to do this interview all by herself? Alison tried to think of some amusing anecdotes about *Sticks and Stones* that she could share with the audience, but none came to mind.

With just five minutes left till air time, Jamie hurried into the waiting room, looking a little frazzled.

"I cannot, absolutely cannot wait until I learn to drive!" she exclaimed.

Life in Los Angeles didn't really start until you could get places on your own. Alison had always been lucky either her mother or the housekeeper had been around to take her wherever she wanted to go.

"Couldn't get a ride?" Alison asked sympathetically.

"No. My mother was supposed to drop me off, but the

car had muffler problems. I should have asked the studio to send a car.''

Alison always felt embarrassed riding around in a studio limo, but Jamie really enjoyed all the fuss. As Jamie ran a comb through her thick copper-colored hair, Alison watched her. Jamie was a mass of contradictions. How could someone so talented be so insecure? True, her family life hadn't been that hot, but Jamie just needed to get past that. She was on a hit TV show. Shouldn't that count for something? Then Alison reconsidered. She was on the same show, and that fact wasn't helping her self-confidence much at the moment either.

''Have you met the host yet?'' Jamie asked, shoving the comb back into her purse.

Alison shook her head. ''All I got was this cup of coffee and orders to wait.''

''Sometimes a production assistant will interview you before the show and ask you questions. I guess this time we're going to wing it.''

''Wing it,'' Alison repeated dully.

The door opened and a short, slight man with a gray crewcut bustled into the room. ''Don Powell. I'm the host of *On the Scene.*'' He stuck out his hand and gave each girl a perfunctory shake.

Alison murmured hello, but Don cut her off mid-syllable. ''Come on, let's head into the studio.''

As they walked down the hall, Don rattled off the topics he wanted to cover. ''Why do you think the show got off to such a good start? What's it like to work with established stars like Ben and Donna? Any big heads on the set?''

Even Jamie was looking a little discombobulated by the time Don settled them in the studio.

To calm herself, Alison glanced around the studio. It was a lot nicer than she pictured a radio studio being— paneled walls, plush carpeting and chairs, even a rosewood table on which the microphones sat. Maybe things were different at funky AM stations, but this place was top of the line. *Well,* Alison thought, *that makes sense.* The publicity department at the network would hardly put them on some fly-by-night program.

"We're almost done with the news," Don said, putting on his earphones and gesturing the girls to do the same. Alison tried to watch what Jamie was doing, but her fingers were so slippery with sweat, it took her a couple of tries to adjust the phones. She got them into place just as the station jingle finished and Don pushed the microphone closer.

"Well, good morning folks, it's eight-thirty in bright, balmy L.A. And brightening up my morning are two dazzling redheads. You've been under a barrel if you haven't heard of the hot new TV show *Sticks and Stones.* Two of the stars, Jamie O'Leary and Alison Blake, are here. They're going to give us all the inside dope on their program, and what it's like to be teen idols.

Teen idols? Alison reacted with a start. Since when were they teen idols?

Don turned to her expectantly. "Alison Blake, you're the new kid on the block. Never even worked on TV before, right?"

Alison snapped to attention. "Uh, right."

"Well, don't keep us in the dark." Don frowned, as if

she should have realized he'd want more. "How did you get the job?"

Alison knew that she should tell the whole amusing story. She had been at the casting call just so her friend Dana wouldn't have to go alone. The only reason she got a shot at the role was because Dan Greenspan thought she was just the type he was looking for. But that long anecdote seemed more than she could handle. So all she said, in a high, tight voice, was, "Dan Greenspan, the producer, chose me."

She's choking, Jamie thought to herself. She knew even a little bit of dead air time on the radio could sound like a lot, so she jumped in. "Alison wasn't even at Dan's office for the audition."

"No?" Don asked, sensing a story. He turned to Alison. "Then why were you picked?"

"I had red hair," Alison squeaked.

Both Don and Jamie waited for her to proceed, but Alison just sat there, so Jamie finished the story. Wrapping up, she turned to Alison and asked, "It was a real surprise, wasn't it, Alison?"

Alison finally found her tongue. "Oh, yes, it was the last thing I was expecting. I still can't believe it's happened." *There,* she thought with relief. *Two sentences.* No one could think she wasn't holding up her end now.

Apparently, Don Powell could. He immediately asked how being on the show had changed her life.

A million thoughts flooded Alison's head—so many, she couldn't really pick one to share with the audience. Finally, she settled for a limp, "Oh, it's not so different."

After that, Don basically ignored Alison and directed his questions to Jamie, who seemed to delight in replying in fresh and funny ways.

"So is there much squabbling on the set?" Don asked.

"You mean are we really throwing sticks and stones at each other?" she replied with a giggle. "No. I guess we get along as well as a bunch of actors can, considering we all have reasonably sized egos."

Alison watched Jamie in amazement. She might have been sitting in the commissary chatting with cast and crew, not talking live on the radio to a guy she had never seen before.

Finally, Don came back to Alison. He must have realized excluding her any more would have seemed rude.

"Alison, any plans to move on to movies?"

"Oh, no. I just got on television." Alison didn't know what else she could add to that. It was such a stupid question.

"And I'm sure you'll be on it for a long, long time," Don said smoothly. "We're going to break for the weather and traffic report, so I thank you, Jamie O'Leary and Alison Blake, for joining us this morning."

The red On Air light went off in the studio, and Don turned to them. "Jamie," he said enthusiastically, "you make a great interview."

"Thanks," Jamie said.

To Alison, Don only muttered, "I appreciate your coming, Alison."

As soon as they were out of Don's earshot, Alison turned to Jamie and said glumly, "I was a major-league flop."

Jamie wasn't sure how to answer that. She was secretly thrilled to find one thing that Alison didn't excel at. On the other hand, Alison looked so woebegone, a person would have to be pretty hardhearted to agree that she'd sat there like a lump of mashed potatoes.

Jamie decided to walk a fine line. "It was your first time. You'll get better."

Alison tried to believe Jamie, but she suspected it was all nice words. "The next time will be television, Jamie. If I can't handle an interview where I'm totally invisible, how am I going to manage when a couple of million people are watching?"

Jamie had no answer for that.

"Maybe I should just tell Mr. Greenspan I can't do it," Alison suggested unhappily. "Maybe I ought to stay home."

Once again, Jamie was torn. For a few marvelous seconds, a vision of going on tour without Alison flashed through her mind's eye. All that attention going straight to her. Jamie O'Leary in the spotlight, chatting on television. And gloriously gowned, at the American Choice Awards. Standing up on that stage without Alison joined to her hip. Then she came back to earth. It was doubtful the network would let one of their young stars voluntarily take the backseat.

"Dan won't let you. Everything's all arranged. It would look weird if the plans changed now," Jamie said.

Alison was silent for a few seconds; then she nodded her agreement. "I guess you're right."

"Don't worry so much," Jamie advised. "Who knows,

maybe live television will turn out to be a piece of cake for you. Now that you've gotten your feet wet, things are bound to get better.''

Alison gave her a look of sheer disbelief.

''All right, maybe I'm being a little optimistic, but who would have thought you'd wind up a big television star in the first place?''

Alison swallowed hard and nodded. ''I guess I'll just have to keep in mind the words of my old algebra teacher, Mrs. Dumont. Whenever we were all staring blankly at the blackboard, when we couldn't understand a word, she always said, 'Let it be a challenge to you.' '' Alison sighed. ''I have a feeling I'm about to face my biggest challenge yet.''

''You sounded just like you were in the next room,'' Mrs. O'Leary said. For about the fifth time.

Although Jamie was glad her mother was so excited about her radio appearance, she was getting just a little tired of her mother's praise. She hadn't stopped talking about the show since she got home from work.

''Mom, this can't be the first time you've listened to the radio. Transmission's great, probably has been since 1930.''

Mrs. O'Leary ignored that comment. ''I bet Alison felt terrible.''

Up until now all her mother's observations had been about Jamie's performance. However, since Mrs. O'Leary had brought it up, Jamie was eager to hear what she had to say about Alison.

"Did she sound as nervous as she actually was?"

"She sounded nervous when she actually said anything, which wasn't too often."

"Alison's pretty worried about the tour."

"Well, she ought to be," Mrs. O'Leary said. "Now, what can I fix you for dinner? Elsie's sleeping over at your father's so we can have whatever we want. I could make some tacos, or maybe we should just order a pizza.

Jamie's stomach turned over. She was both craving food and repulsed by the thought. The only way she had been able to get through the last weeks was by trying to avoid food altogether. Usually, it was pretty easy at home. Elsie was so finicky about food, the menus tended to fish sticks, peanut butter, and spaghetti. Jamie usually made herself a sandwich, which she said she was going to eat while she studied her lines. Then she put most of it in the garbage.

"So, which will it be?" her mother prompted.

Jamie got off the couch and started rifling through a carton of books that was still waiting to be unpacked. "I'm not really that hungry."

"You never seem to be hungry lately," Mrs. O'Leary said.

Jamie could feel her mother's eyes piercing into her back. "I eat a lot at the studio," Jamie answered without turning around.

"Then how come you're looking so thin?" her mother asked bluntly.

Pasting a smile on her face, Jamie faced her mother. "I've been dieting a little. Don't you know the camera adds ten pounds?"

"Seems to me like you've already lost those ten pounds. Jamie, are you on some crazy diet?"

The question hung in the air. Fortunately for Jamie the doorbell broke the silence.

"I'll get it," Jamie said quickly. "David," she said with surprise. How did he know her address, she wondered.

As if in answer to her unspoken question, David said, "Your sister told me where you live. I asked when I saw her in the park today."

"Oh. Would you like to come in?"

"That's what I'm here for," David said cheerfully.

Jamie quickly introduced David to her mother, who she could tell was scrutinizing him quite carefully.

"Nice to meet you," David said. He noticed Mrs. O'Leary's apron. "I guess I'm too late."

"Too late for what?" Jamie asked.

"I wanted to see if you could grab a burger with me."

Jamie quickly calculated. On the one hand, she wasn't sure she wanted to spend time with David. On the other, if she went with him, she could eat away from her mother's prying eyes. There was only one decision. "Can I go, Mom?"

Her mother smiled understandingly. "Sure, honey, you go ahead and have a good time."

When they got outside, Jamie was surprised to see a perfectly respectable car parked in front of the apartment. Somehow she expected David would drive an old junker. Of course, this car was nothing like the sports car Steve Kaye drove. Steve, who was on vacation with his parents, was a really nice guy. She had gone to his high school prom with him. But it had only been one date. She didn't have to feel guilty about going out with David.

She slid into the car beside him. "So where do you want to go?"

"The Bun?" David suggested. The drive-in was a local favorite.

"All right." Jamie figured she could order something and just nibble. At least David wouldn't scrutinize her eating habits.

After they had placed their order with a waitress on roller skates, David leaned back in his seat and said, "I heard you on the radio this morning."

"You did?" Jamie asked with surprise. "I didn't think you were the type to listen to talk radio."

"What do you think I would listen to?"

"Heavy metal?" Jamie suggested.

"That too. But I do try to catch *On the Scene* every once in a while. Don Powell's usually up on the entertainment news."

Jamie was puzzled. "Why do you care about that sort of stuff?"

"What? You think you're the only person involved in the business?"

"You mean you're in show business?"

"Well, don't look so shocked, Jamie. We can't all be television stars, but a few of us lowly types do get work, too."

Jamie was finding this a little hard to take in. Almost immediately, she became suspicious. Was David one of those aspiring actors who tried to take advantage of every contact that came his way?

"And not all of us want to be in tel-e-vis-ion," David said disdainfully.

Jamie unconsciously pulled away from him. "Excuse me, what's wrong with television?"

David hesitated. "Maybe we shouldn't talk about this. I didn't invite you here to rag on you about your job."

"No, please," Jamie said icily. "Obviously, you don't think much of TV. Why not?"

David looked as if he knew he couldn't get out of this. "Television's all right, I guess. A little mindless. But you can't call acting on television *real* acting."

"Why not?"

"The scripts are hackneyed. You have no range of emotion." David warmed to his subject. "It's the same thing week after week. Movies aren't much better. Action movies, so-called thrillers, sex stuff. Who needs it?"

"Sorry you consider the state of entertainment so bad." David shrugged.

"What kind of acting do *you* do?" Jamie hoped David noticed the sarcasm dripping from her voice.

"The only real acting today is in the theater."

"And am I to take that to mean you've acted on stage or are you just hoping to someday?"

"I've had a few parts," David said.

"Like what?"

"I performed at the Shakespeare Festival."

Jamie cocked her head. "Let me guess, you played Romeo."

"Not that time, but I will."

"So, what part did you have?"

David hesitated. Then he said, "I was in the crowd scenes in *Julius Caesar*."

"And where can I see you performing now?" Jamie asked.

David's face reddened. "Right now, I'm just auditioning."

"Oh," Jamie said softly. "Auditioning."

"It's Shakespeare anyway. Not a sitcom."

The waitress brought the food. David handed Jamie her cola and the burger she had ordered.

"I don't think I'm hungry," she snapped.

"Well, I am," David said, biting his hot dog.

Jamie waited until David had had a few more bites. Then she insisted, "I really have to be getting home. *I* have lines to study."

Dave finished his hot dog, crumpled his garbage, and threw it into the paper bag. "It can't be that hard," he muttered as he threw the car into reverse.

The ride home was silent. Jamie didn't know when she had had such a rotten time. The only good part was that she had only had two bites of her hamburger, and no one cared a bit.

Chapter 4

"Alison, you're packing more for a few days in New York than I'm taking for the cruise."

Alison tried to stuff one more pair of shoes into the suitcase sitting on her bed. "But no one's going to be looking at you."

Mrs. Blake laughed. "I hope that's not true."

"You know what I mean, Mom," Alison responded distractedly.

Mrs. Blake put her arm around her daughter's shoulder and led her over to a chair.

"Mom, I don't have time," Alison protested. "The plane is—"

"Going to leave in about four hours," her mother finished. "You're almost packed—you would be packed, if you'd just quit adding items. I think what you need to do is relax for a few minutes. Should I have Estelle make you a cup of tea?"

Alison had to admit it felt pretty good to sit down. "No, I don't want any tea."

"Is there anything you do want?"

Yeah, Alison thought. *To go in my bedroom and put my head under the covers.* But she kept that comment to herself. She felt like she had already whined too much to her parents. When she came home after her *On the Scene* flop, she moped around the house. Her parents had been supportive. As usual, they were there saying all the right things, telling her that once she had a few more interviews under her belt, she'd be just fine.

For a while, Alison had let herself be convinced, but here, a few hours away from a trip to New York, all her doubts were firmly in place.

"Are there any last-minute errands you want to run?" Mrs. Blake asked.

"There is one thing I've been thinking about doing," Alison admitted. "Calling Dana."

Dana Jones was the friend that Alison had accompanied to the audition, and Dana had never been too happy about Alison's good fortune. Only when Dana had gotten a job as an extra on *Sticks and Stones* had she begun to forgive Alison for stealing what she considered to be "her part."

But to Alison's dismay, Dana hadn't been satisfied with her extra role. She tried to make something more out of it, and as soon as her episode had been taped, she immediately wanted to know if her role was going to be made into a regular. It had taken some blunt talk from Jamie to get through to Dana, and in the process, Dana had gotten awfully mad. Dana hadn't spoken to Alison since.

"I've tried not to pry about this, Alison. I know you and

Dana didn't see eye to eye on the set, but you have been friends for such a long time."

"Of course, Dana hasn't made any effort to call me," Alison pointed out, trying not to sound bitter, "but I do feel bad about the fight."

"Then maybe you should call. Someone's got to make the first move. Why not you?"

"You think?"

"Nothing ventured, nothing gained."

"All right," Alison decided. "I'll give it a shot."

Mrs. Blake discreetly left the room, and Alison dialed Dana's number. She almost hoped that Dana wouldn't answer, but after one ring she picked up the phone.

"Hi, Dana, it's Alison."

"Oh. Hi, Ali."

Alison could almost feel the frost forming on the phone. "It's been such a long time . . ."

"I know how busy you've been. After all, stardom does take up time," Dana said sarcastically.

"Come on, Dana. Can't we forget about this? After all, you did get to be on the show."

"And you got mad because I wanted to be on it again."

"That's not true. I have no control over who gets picked for the regular cast. Can't we forget about this?"

"Oh, all right," Dana said sullenly.

Well, it's a start, Alison thought to herself. "So what have you been up to?"

"Just the usual. With school out, I'm auditioning a lot. But with just one piddling appearance as an extra, I can't even get agents interested, let alone casting directors."

Dana wasn't making this very easy, but Alison decided she wasn't going to take the bait. "Well, are there any new guys on the scene?"

There was a slight hesitation on Dana's part. "Actually, I've gone out a few times with Brad."

Alison felt a slight shock tingle through her body. It was more surprise than jealousy. Brad sure didn't waste much time, Alison thought. And she wouldn't have guessed that Dana was Brad's type.

"Alison?" For the first time, Dana sounded a little nervous.

"It's no problem, Dana," Alison said, trying to sound cool.

"Really?"

"No. Brad and I are old news. I have no problem with you dating him."

"That's great," Dana said, relieved.

"Maybe we can get together when I get back," Alison said.

"Where are you going?"

Alison quickly filled Dana in on the publicity tour.

"That sounds exciting," Dana said unenthusiastically. She didn't say she'd be watching any of the shows Alison had named.

Alison was a little hurt, but not surprised. "My plane leaves in a little while, so I'd better get going."

"Okay, I'll catch you later then," Dana promised.

Hanging up the phone, Alison wondered if Dana really meant it.

"How did it go?" Mrs. Blake asked, coming into the bedroom.

Alison sighed. "All right, I guess. She's dating Brad."

"Do you mind?" her mother asked sympathetically.

"Not really. It's just that my life has undergone such amazing changes in the last few months."

Mrs. Blake nodded. "Life has a way of doing that."

The next couple of hours were filled with last minute odds and ends. Alison didn't want her parents to drive her to the airport, but they insisted. By the time the Blakes said good-bye at the gate, Alison was sure they had given her enough advice for three trips to New York. Everything from "Watch your purse" to "Don't talk to strangers." Alison had to remind her parents that talking to strangers was all she was going to be doing for the next couple of days. On television, yet.

Finally, though, after a flurry of kisses and wishing each other a good trip, Alison was alone. Cindy Vargas, the production assistant from the show, would be on the same flight, along with Mike and Jamie, but so far none of them had shown up yet.

Alison glanced around the airport. She had flown with her parents a million times, but never alone. Flying didn't make her nervous exactly, but it wasn't her favorite thing. Before, she had always had her parents to calm her down if the ride got bumpy. She hoped today's flight would be smooth.

"Hi, babe." Mike put his hand on Alison's shoulder. "Ready for the Big Apple?"

Alison gave him a small smile. "Is anyone ever ready for that?"

"It's not like we're coming from Podunk here. L.A.'s a big city, in case you haven't noticed."

"Tell it to my parents."

"Hey," Mike said, looking at his ticket. "Do you want to see if we can sit together?"

Alison laughed. "Funny you should mention it."

By the time they had finished checking in, Jamie and Cindy had arrived.

"You'd better get in line," Mike told them. "I heard the reservation clerk say that the plane is going to be full."

"Hey, maybe we'll all get bumped from the flight," Alison said in a mock-hopeful tone.

"Forget it," Cindy said. A tiny brunette whose pixie haircut made her look even younger, Cindy was obviously making it clear that she was in charge. It was her responsibility to make sure that everything ran smoothly in New York, to get them safely from one event to another.

"I'm only kidding," Alison replied meekly.

"That's good. We've got a full schedule in New York, starting with that fashion shoot bright and early tomorrow morning. We can't afford to be even one second late."

The fashion shoot. Jamie had been thinking of that with a mixture of delight and dread. She knew she had lost enough weight so that she wouldn't be totally embarrassed around Alison or a lot of skinny models. But Alison did have a natural elegance. Jamie was worried she still wouldn't measure up.

Jamie waved her ticket. "I'm going to check in." Having something practical to do would keep her mind off the fashion shoot, at least for a little while. She had hopes of a long, leisurely journey sitting next to Mike, but as usual she was too late. From the cozy way Mike and Alison had advised her and Cindy to get in line, it was clear that they had already chosen seats together.

The reservation clerk checked Jamie's ticket. "You're in first class, Miss O'Leary."

Jamie nodded. She was totally thrilled to be flying first class. She had barely flown at all, and then just for *The Happydale Girls*. If she had flown first class then, she had been too young to notice it. Now, however, she was determined to pay attention to every marvelous detail. She'd ignore Alison and Mike and just luxuriate.

Even Alison, who had flown first class before, was pretty impressed with the service. The flight attendants greeted them by name, and were serving them shrimp-puff hors d'oeuvres before the plane even took off. She looked over at Mike, who was buckling his seat belt.

"These seats are huge," Mike said, reclining.

"They're sure more comfortable than your motorcycle."

Mike shook his head. "No more. I bought myself a car yesterday. I'm having a little custom work done, and it will be ready when I get back."

"Tell me about it," Alison said.

Mike talked enthusiastically about his car throughout the takeoff. "I suppose you have a couple of cars at your house."

Alison nodded.

"You'll be turning sixteen soon. That'll be cool, having your pick of cars. Or maybe you'll just buy one of your own."

"I'm so busy at the studio," Alison said. "I can't imagine when I'm going to have time to learn to drive."

"Well, we'll fix that when we get back," Mike smiled. "I'll teach you to drive."

"Oh, that would be too much trouble," Alison protested.

"Why take lessons from some driving school when you have a real expert offering to teach you?"

As Mike smiled and pushed back his wayward lock of hair, Alison could feel herself melting a little. She always thought Mike was cute, but she didn't think she had a real chance with him. Now here he was offering to teach her to drive. He wouldn't do that if he didn't like her, would he?

"That might be fun," Alison said, smiling back brightly.

They chatted all through the flight, stopping only to have the filet mignon that was served for dinner. After the flight attendants removed the trays, Mike said, "Well, I think this trip is off to a pretty good start."

"I hope this isn't the last good thing that happens."

"Why would you say something like that?"

"I guess you didn't hear me on the radio," Alison said quietly.

"It didn't go so well?"

"I froze," Alison admitted. "If it hadn't been for Jamie jumping in, Don Powell would have been talking to himself."

"I can't believe it was as bad as all that," Mike said.

"Believe it."

"All right, so maybe you had a trial by fire, but now that

you have some experience under your belt, you'll do fine next time out.''

"You sound like my parents," Alison told him.

"Parents can be right sometimes."

"Let's hope you all are."

"I suppose Jamie was thrilled to be center stage," Mike commented.

Alison shrugged. "It wasn't Jamie's fault she was on the air with a clam.''

"Jamie's been jealous of you since you walked on the set," Mike said.

"I know Jamie thinks I'm too privileged or something, but she's been better lately. She even helped me when Dana was being such a drag.''

"I still wouldn't trust her as far as I could throw her," Mike muttered.

"Mike, even for an actor you're being dramatic." Alison looked at him quizzically. "Do you know something I don't?''

For a second, Mike seemed as if he wanted to tell Alison something, but all he said was, "Just watch your back.''

Chapter 5

"What a gorgeous room!" Alison exclaimed.

"One of the nicest in the hotel," Cindy agreed.

"I didn't know Alison and I were going to be sharing," Jamie said a little petulantly.

"You have a whole suite," Cindy pointed out. "And there's a king-size bed for each of you in the bedroom. I don't think you'll be bumping into each other."

Jamie knew she should be thrilled about their glorious digs. The living room, complete with minibar, and bedroom combined were as big as her old apartment, and the view of the New York skyline from the many windows was breathtaking.

But Jamie was feeling out of sorts. She had taken too much advantage of flying first class. She had promised herself before taking off that she would only nibble at the food, but she hadn't eaten much all day and she couldn't restrain herself. A few peanuts and a cola had led to the filet mignon and cheesecake. Now she was feeling hopelessly fat. And with the photo shoot coming up first thing in the morning!

"It's fine," Jamie said, scanning the suite. "It's more than fine."

"Well, good. I'll let you two get settled. I arranged for the luggage to be delivered from the airport to the hotel, and it will be brought up as soon as it arrives."

"I couldn't believe we didn't have to wait around for our bags," Alison said. "That was the height of luxury."

"Get used to it," Cindy laughed. "By the way, I've left a very early wake-up call for you, so as soon as your stuff gets here, crawl into your jammies and get some rest. You've got to look as fresh as little flowers tomorrow."

I'll probably look as fat as a little piggy, Jamie thought glumly.

"Can I talk to you for a second, Alison?" Cindy asked.

Jamie disappeared into the bedroom. "What's wrong?" Alison asked.

"Things didn't go too well on the radio show."

Alison felt herself flush with embarrassment. She should have guessed this would come up.

"Dan mentioned we could get you a coach," Cindy continued.

"I . . . I wasn't feeling very well that morning. I'll do better," Alison said a little desperately.

"Well, don't forget it's an option. But you have to let me know so I can arrange it."

"No, it's okay."

"Get a good night's sleep," Cindy said sympathetically. "I'm sure you'll do fine." Then Cindy said good night and Alison wandered into the bedroom.

"What did she want?" Jamie asked from her bed, where she was lying.

"Nothing. Just wanted to go over the schedule." Alison changed the subject. "Do you want to watch some television?"

"I don't know," Jamie replied. "Maybe I'll go out for a walk."

"A walk! Now?"

"It's not that late," Jamie said grumpily. Maybe there was a chance she could walk off a few calories.

"I don't think that's a good idea. Cindy said we should go to bed."

"Cindy doesn't run everything."

"Actually, she does, Jamie, at least as far as we're concerned. But if you really have to go for a walk, maybe you'd better call Mike. I don't think you should go alone."

Now there's an idea, Jamie thought.

A knock at the door interrupted them. Alison went into the living room and after cautiously asking who was there, she let the bellboy in.

"Where would you like me to put these?" he asked politely.

"Oh, in the bedroom, I guess," Alison replied. Then she looked at the bags more closely. "Where are the rest of them?"

"The rest?"

"My bags aren't here," Alison said, her voice rising a little.

Jamie came out of the bedroom. "She's right. All of these are mine."

''These were all I was given to bring up. But let me go downstairs and check again.''

Alison watched with dismay as the bellboy took the bags into the bedroom. She turned to Jamie. ''You don't think my bags could be lost, do you?''

''Nah. They just got a little mixed up downstairs, that's all.''

Alison sat down on the brocade couch. ''All my stuff is in there.''

''Hey, if worst comes to worst, you can always buy more clothes.''

Alison looked at her with stricken eyes. ''It's not just the clothes. All my good-luck stuff was in there.''

''Good-luck stuff?''

Alison knew that it sounded babyish, but she didn't care. ''A charm bracelet my parents gave me when I was eleven, and this stuffed bear I've had since I was a baby, Tippy . . .''

Tippy the stuffed bear, Jamie thought. *How adorable.*

''And the shoes I was wearing when I went to the audition with Dana . . .''

''Okay, I get it, but don't sweat it yet, Alison.''

The bellboy left and the moments ticked by. Jamie turned on the television, and Alison tried to watch, but she kept waiting for a knock at the door.

''I'm sure the bellboy will be bringing up your bags any second,'' Jamie said.

Finally, the bellboy returned, but he was empty-handed.

''Sorry, but we can't find any other bags for this suite.''

Alison looked at Jamie, stricken.

"All right, calm down. I'll call Cindy. She'll know what to do."

Jamie had to hand it to Cindy. She was certainly a take-charge person. She called the manager of the hotel, the courier service that was supposed to deliver the bags, and the airlines. But all her forcefulness did not make the bags appear. After hanging up from her final call, Cindy said, "Well, I guess your bags are among the missing."

"Oh, no," Alison groaned.

"Now, come on. They will turn up. They always do. You just may not have them for tomorrow. I'll call downstairs and get you a toothbrush and the other stuff you'll need tonight." She turned to Jamie. "Do you have anything Alison can wear tomorrow?"

No one but Jamie seemed to appreciate the irony in poor Jamie O'Leary lending rich Alison Blake clothes, so all Jamie said was, "I think so."

"All she'll need is jeans and a sweater. The magazine is going to have all sorts of terrific stuff for the shoot."

"Jeans?" Alison asked doubtfully.

"We'll just explain that the airlines lost your stuff. Everyone will be very sympathetic," Cindy said. "And look at the bright side. You've just picked up a fresh interview topic."

The trio went into the bedroom, and Jamie opened her suitcase. She pulled out a cropped sweater embroidered with butterflies. It was one of the items that the costume department provided for the trip, and one she wasn't overly fond of. "How's this?"

"Cute," Cindy said approvingly. "What about jeans?"

Jamie found a denim skirt and tossed it to Alison. "How about this?"

Alison checked the size. "With a belt, it should be okay."

Jamie didn't think a belt was going to be necessary and felt insulted that Alison did, but she kept her mouth shut.

"Good," Cindy said with relief. "Then everything's settled. I think you two should get to bed. Alison, no more worrying about your bags," she ordered.

"Okay. Thank you, Cindy," Alison said.

After they said good night, Alison and Jamie dutifully got ready for bed.

"I don't feel very well," Alison said.

"You're just upset. I'm sure you'll be fine."

"I don't think I'll be able to sleep."

Jamie was torn. She did feel bad that Alison's bags were missing, but she had to admit a certain, secret spark of pleasure. If Alison was discombobulated tomorrow, maybe Jamie'd have a chance to shine at the shoot.

The next morning, when the wake-up call came at the crack of dawn, Jamie was surprised to see Alison already up.

"How long have you been awake?" she asked with a yawn.

"The correct question should be, did I sleep at all."

Jamie peered at Alison. She did look pretty tired.

"I was just so wired, I couldn't fall asleep."

"So you were up all night?"

Alison shrugged. "Oh, maybe I dozed off a little."

"Well, one night without sleep won't hurt. I'll call room service and get us some coffee. That should help."

Alison smiled tremulously. "Tell them to make it strong."

Forty-five minutes later they were climbing into a limo to take them to the shoot.

Cindy looked at Alison critically. "Are you okay?"

"I guess." She explained about her night.

Cindy sighed. "We've got the best makeup people in New York waiting for us. I guess we're going to find out just how talented they are."

Alison knew it wasn't intentional, but Cindy had just succeeded in undermining whatever confidence Alison had left. How could she waltz into this shoot—in borrowed clothes, no less—looking so bad?

Jamie wasn't feeling much better. The bloated feeling she had gone to sleep with hadn't gone away in the morning. She could feel the anger rising within her. All the hard work she had done dieting, and now this. It just wasn't fair.

As the limo pulled out into the street, Alison got her first daylight view of New York City. Despite the early hour, the city was already alive. Pedestrians hurried to work, drivers honked, and taxis darted around anyone too timid to charge through a traffic light.

Craning her neck, Alison looked up at all the tall buildings crowded together. Los Angeles had its share of skyscrapers, but they were more spread apart. Alison couldn't believe New York's filled block after block.

The taxi scooted downtown along Fifth Avenue. Alison caught sight of some famous stores. Then the buildings thinned out a little. The cab turned into an area that seemed to be mostly warehouses.

"This is where the shoot is going to be?" Jamie asked with surprise.

"Lots of studios are here," Cindy responded. "We're in the heart of the fashion district."

They got out at an old, squat building and went upstairs in a creaky elevator. Alison and Jamie exchanged looks. Was Cindy sure they had the right place?

But when the elevator doors opened, it was as though they had stepped into a different world. A bright reception area with incredibly high ceilings greeted them. Covering the walls were gigantic black-and-white photographs of models, women and men in all sorts of exotic poses.

A receptionist with spiked blond hair and lots of black eye makeup looked up when they entered and assessed them coolly. "Can I help you?"

Cindy took over, and once she explained who they were, the receptionist's attitude changed dramatically. *"Sticks and Stones,* of course," she cooed. "I should have recognized you. Let me buzz Edmund."

"Edmund Brooks is one of the best photographers in New York City," Cindy whispered.

I'm going to need the best, both Alison and Jamie thought.

In a few seconds, a short, muscular man with a salt-and-pepper beard and hair appeared at the receptionist's desk. "Hello," he greeted them, shaking all of their hands. "How are you all?"

"Nervous," Jamie admitted.

"My bags never arrived," Alison said, wanting to make that point immediately. "That's why I'm wearing Jamie's clothes," she babbled.

Edmund smiled. "Don't let it throw you. We've got all sorts of clothes you can wear. Now, let's go into the studio. I've got my team ready to do your hair and makeup."

They were taken into the studio, a brightly lighted room with overstuffed leather furniture. A tall young man and a woman dressed all in black were talking in the center of it.

Edmund quickly made the introductions. Lisa was in charge of the makeup, and Tony was the hairdresser.

Edmund ran his fingers through Alison's hair. "A little shorter, don't you think?"

"Shorter?" Alison faltered.

"Just a little," Tony assured her.

"I like Jamie's French braid," Edmund continued. "Let's leave it, but do something interesting with hair decorations."

There was a discussion about the type of makeup with Lisa that went right over the girls' heads.

"All right," Edmund said. "We're clear on that. Now let's look at the costumes."

Later, Alison and Jamie agreed that picking out their costumes for the shoot was about the best way they had ever spent an hour.

Unlike their costumes on *Sticks and Stones,* these outfits looked as if they came from the fanciest fashion houses.

Pierce, the young woman who had helped select them explained, "Edmund wants different looks for the various shots. She held up an incredibly hot-looking silk camisole top and wrap shorts outfit. "This for an everyday kind of thing. And this"—she picked up a short, full, strapless party dress in hot pink—"this for evening."

"I'd like to have an evening where I could wear this," Jamie murmured.

Cindy smiled. "You will. Don't forget the American Choice Awards."

"Somebody slap me," Jamie said. "Looking at these clothes really makes me believe that the awards show is going to happen."

"Me, too," Alison added with a gulp.

Cindy turned to Pierce. "Maybe if we can find two really great-looking dresses, we can borrow them for the show."

Pierce nodded. "I don't see why not. I'm sure the designers would love to have their dresses shown off on a big television award show."

Jamie and Alison went off to separate dressing rooms to try on the various outfits that Pierce suggested for them. Alison first put on an ice-white sarong dress. It hugged her lean body.

Pierce stuck her head into the dressing room. "Oh, that's a keeper. Now try on that peach evening gown. Maybe it will work for the awards show."

Alison dutifully changed, but when she saw the dress on, she wrinkled her nose. "I don't like the color."

"Me either," Pierce agreed. "I think redheads often stay away from colors they really could wear, like red, but this shade does clash with your hair. Let me see if Jamie has anything in her dressing room that would do more for you than this."

Pierce walked over to Jamie's dressing room. Jamie wasn't wearing any of the great clothes. She was just standing in her underwear, staring at herself intently in the mirror.

"Hey, we're not going to be modeling underwear here," Pierce said with a smile.

Jamie turned around, startled. "Oh."

Pierce looked at her shrewdly. "Feeling fat?"

"Do I look fat?" Jamie asked, horrified.

Pierce stepped into the dressing room and looked her over. "Not really. You are the curvy type, naturally, aren't you?"

"I guess," Jamie shrugged.

"But you want to be the thin type, like Alison," Pierce guessed.

"How did you know?" Jamie grabbed a blouse and threw it over her.

"I see models all day long. Not many of them think they're thin enough."

"I have been on a diet," Jamie admitted. She looked at herself with dissatisfaction. "But it's not working fast enough."

"You're pretty thin," Pierce said.

"But I ate too much last night." Jamie grabbed a tiny roll of stomach. "And now there's this."

Pierce shrugged. "I've seen worse."

"And better. Like Alison, I'll bet."

"Alison is definitely the natural model type," Pierce agreed. "She's tall, high waisted, and slim, but that doesn't mean there's anything wrong with your build."

"I want to be thinner," Jamie insisted. "I've just got to get down." Her insistent tone sounded a little strange even to her own ears. This dieting thing had started because she wanted to look better in her clothes, more like Alison. But then, without her even realizing it, the dieting had taken on a life of its own. She seemed to spend a lot of her time lately thinking about what she ate and what she didn't. If she didn't eat much, she was pleased with herself, and if she cheated, like last night, she was furious.

Jamie told herself she'd stop thinking about dieting once she got to her desired weight. Unfortunately, that always seemed to be a pound or two away from where she was.

"Well," Pierce warned, "don't let this dieting get out of hand. I'm sure you've heard of anorexia and bulimia."

"I don't do anything like that," Jamie said quickly. "I mean, you know . . ."

"Throw up," Pierce finished for her. "Or take laxatives."

Jamie made a face. "I wouldn't do that."

"But you can diet to excess. That's anorexia."

"What's excess?" Jamie asked flippantly. "I mean if it works . . ."

"You can start losing your hair from too much dieting. Your periods can stop . . ."

"Oh, yuck."

"Just don't overdo it," Pierce repeated.

"I won't," Jamie said, subdued.

"Your figure may not have been a model's, but it was probably cute and curvy." Pierce smiled a little. "The kind guys like. So why not relax and not worry about getting too thin?"

After Pierce had closed the door to the dressing room,

Jamie took off the blouse she had put on and continued to examine her body. She could see her ribs, Jamie noted with delight.

But a tiny voice inside her said that Pierce was right. It was silly to put so much effort into losing weight when she hadn't been all that heavy to start out with.

Drowning out that voice, however, was a much stronger feeling. She couldn't explain it to Pierce, but dieting made her feel as if she was in control. Maybe she couldn't decide how many lines she'd have in a particular script, or whether her parents would get back together, but the one thing she could do—most of the time, anyway—was to choose how much food she would put in her mouth.

Jamie turned and looked at herself from a rear view. Besides, she wasn't too thin. She was just starting to look really great. A few more pounds ought to do it. Then she'd be perfect.

Chapter 6

The rest of the morning went by like a dream. Not that it was all that easy. The girls found out that what everyone said about modeling was true—it was hard work.

By the end of the session, every muscle in Alison's face was stiff from smiling. Jamie had twisted into so many poses that she felt like she was turning into a pretzel.

The session had started out in the studio with the girls in everyday clothes. The idea of the shoot was to take two young actresses through their busy day. Both Alison and Jamie had to laugh a little at this. So far, they hadn't had a day where they'd worn silk day clothes, dressy dinner outfits, and glamorous evening gowns.

When they tentatively entered the studio, Alison and Jamie had just stood around, waiting for someone to tell them what to do. Edmund looked up from his discussion with Pierce and walked over to them, a smile on his face. "You look fabulous. Now, have either of you done any modeling before?"

The girls shook their heads.

Edmund led them over to a big white cushion in the middle of the studio. "I will try to make this as pleasurable as possible. Sit, and just do what I tell you to."

At first, the girls had been very stiff, and Edmund had to coax them to loosen up.

"Don't think about where you are," Edmund insisted. "Just look at me."

It took a while, but eventually, they relaxed. Posing and turning their heads the way Edmund asked, Alison and Jamie began to feel like real models.

When it was time to be photographed in the evening dresses, Edmund had an idea. "Let's do it outside. Right in front of the building. Two beautiful, ethereal girls in gorgeous gowns in front of gritty city buildings. What a contrast!"

Alison and Jamie exchanged looks. It sounded like a bit too much contrast. In fact, it sounded positively goofy.

But down they trooped, all decked out in their evening gowns, Jamie in a strapless black number with a slit up the side, and Alison wearing a short dress with the balloon skirt that showed off her long legs. The best part of their outfits, though, was the jewelry. Alison didn't dare ask if it was real, but it sure looked as though it was. Bright sapphire earrings and a matching necklace sparkled in the sun. Jamie looked elegant with diamond clusters dangling from her ears. If this was the glamorous side of show business, Alison had to admit she liked it.

She supposed that they would cause a sensation on the street, with the cameras, lights, and entourage, but she had forgotten she was in New York. A few turned heads, but nothing more.

Edmund posed them on the steps of buildings and standing in the middle of the street.

"Isn't this going to look a little weird?" Jamie whispered to Pierce when they were taking a short break. "I mean, Alison and me in the middle of the street . . ."

Pierce smiled. "Wait until you see the proof sheets. You'll think that girls in evening dresses wouldn't be anywhere else."

Jamie wandered over to where Edmund was chatting with Alison. She didn't want to be left out of any important conversations. When she got within earshot, she heard Edmund say to Alison, "If you ever want to leave the television business, Alison, I'm sure you could make it as a model."

Alison blushed. "Oh, I don't think so. I'm totally awkward."

"It's only your first shoot. You'd move into it quite naturally."

Jamie put her head down and moved away. Alison Blake on top again. God, it bugged her. Jamie was sure that she and Alison were doing about equally well in this new experience, but apparently Edmund had seen something in Alison that was totally missing in herself. Why was Alison always two steps ahead of her?

After Edmund finished shooting them in the street, they trooped upstairs to do the final layout, a nighttime scene with Jamie and Alison both in sleepwear.

Alison giggled as she came into the studio wearing

men's style flannel pajamas covered with cowboys on horses. "Aren't these a hoot?" she asked Jamie.

Jamie was still smarting over Edmund's comments, but she didn't want Alison to know that. At least in this particular segment, they were wearing the same pajamas, only Jamie's were shorty style.

"Yeah, they're something."

A bed had appeared in the middle of the studio, covered with stuffed animals. Jamie guessed that Edmund's idea was to show a pair of Cinderellas, dressed in gowns and jewels one moment, in flannel pajamas and hugging toys the next.

Alison wandered over to the bed and picked up one of the toy bears. "This one looks a little like Tippy."

"I don't think you want anybody to hear you talking about your stuffed bear, Alison," Jamie said dryly.

"I know it's silly. I just hope my bags are at the hotel when I get back."

Jamie was hungry and irritable. "It *is* silly," she snapped. "You're going to make all of us look like idiots if you keep talking about all your missing good luck toys."

For a second Alison looked as if Jamie had slapped her. Then she straightened up. "Maybe you're right. I'm not being very professional. Thank you, Jamie," she said through tight lips.

Jamie was surprised at Alison's reaction, but if Alison stopped weeping for lost stuffed bears, Jamie figured it was worth it.

The rest of the shoot went quickly. Jamie was glad when it was finally over. She had been hoping that Edmund might make the same kind of comment to her about modeling that he had made to Alison, but all he said when they left was, "It was a pleasure working with you."

"What do you two want to do about lunch?" Cindy asked as they headed back to the hotel in the limousine.

"I'm not hungry," Jamie said.

"You're not?" Cindy asked in surprise.

To quote Scarlett O'Hara, "I'll never be hungry again." That's what Jamie wanted to say. But all she did was shake her head.

"How about you, Alison?"

"I'm famished," Alison said. "I could eat a horse."

And never gain a pound, Jamie thought grimly.

"New York has all kinds of great restaurants," Cindy said, "but I'm not sure we can find horse anywhere. How about French?"

"Sounds good to me," Alison said as she stepped out of the limo.

"Why don't we take a few minutes to freshen up. Then we can meet downstairs in the lobby. I'll call Mike and he can join us."

"What if my luggage hasn't arrived?" Alison asked.

"Then we'll spend part of the afternoon shopping," Cindy replied with a smile.

A quick look around revealed no bags.

"Oh darn," Alison said, sitting down on her freshly made bed.

"What do you care?" Jamie asked. "Cindy will take you out this afternoon and get you a whole new wardrobe, courtesy of Dan Greenspan's production company."

"Not everything can be that easily replaced," Alison whispered.

Jamie threw up her hands. "So now we're back to the little bear?"

Alison could feel herself getting mad. "What's wrong with you? Why do you have to be such a pain?"

Picking up her hairbrush, Jamie began running it through her bangs with short, hard jabs. "Excuse me."

"You just had the kind of day that every girl dreams of," Alison continued, "and you're acting like you spent it scrubbing floors."

"Maybe some of us had a better day than others," Jamie said, flinging down her brush.

"I don't know what you're talking about," Alison said.

"Never mind," Jamie said, suddenly weary. Maybe she should take a nap this afternoon. At least it would take her mind off food.

There was a knock at the door. Alison opened it and invited Mike and Rodney into the living room.

"So how are the cover girls?" Mike asked.

Jamie came out of the bedroom. "Tired."

"Hungry," Alison added. "Did Cindy call you?"

"Yeah," Mike replied. "She's on the phone with some crisis. She said we should go ahead without her."

"Mike suggested we take the limo and tour New York. Doesn't that sound excellent?" Rodney said.

Alison laughed. Even after all these weeks of working with "the Rodney," she still got a kick out of his very adult way of speaking. "Yes, Rodney, it does." She turned to Jamie. "Do you want to go, too?"

"Well, of course she does," Rodney answered for her. "We're all going."

Even Jamie had to smile at Rodney's enthusiasm. Sometimes he bugged her, but right now, she didn't want to disappoint him. Besides, why make a scene in front of Mike? "I'll go."

"Good, good," Rodney said, happily.

"So how was your interview this morning, Mike?" Alison asked as she picked up her purse.

Mike made a face. "Okay, I guess. It was a call-in show."

"What kinds of questions did they ask?" Jamie wanted to know.

"Oh, the usual stuff, I guess. What it's like to be on a television show. How we get along together."

"Did anyone ask about me?" Rodney demanded.

Mike tousled Rodney's brown hair. "Sorry kid," Mike said sympathetically.

On the way downstairs, Alison and Jamie filled the guys in on the model shoot.

"You mean they actually took pictures of you in your pajamas?" Rodney asked, horrified.

"I was in shorty pajamas," Jamie informed him.

"Well, I certainly hope no one wants to take my picture like that," he replied seriously.

"They won't," Mike assured him.

The limousine was parked in front of the hotel.

"I still can't believe this baby just sits here, waiting for us," Mike said.

Jamie agreed. "Me either."

Mike leaned over to talk to the driver. "Cindy said we could take a little tour of the city."

The driver nodded. "Hop in. I'm Phil," he said. "Where to?"

The kids looked at each other. "Maybe you should decide," Jamie suggested.

"Well now, that's a good idea," Phil said. "No one knows this town better than me. I'll give you a real tour."

Alison settled back in her seat. She was still hoping lunch was on the agenda, but this was going to be so much fun, she didn't mind a few hunger pangs.

Phil stepped on the gas and headed south. "We'll start at Rockefeller Center. There's an ice skating rink there in the winter."

"I've seen pictures of that," Rodney said.

"Here we are. Go out and take a quick look," Phil instructed. "It's a great spot. But don't take too long," he added. "I'll just be circling the block. There's no place to park."

The kids tumbled out of the limo. It was a warm, humid day and there were plenty of people sitting outside. The first thing that struck them was a golden statue of a man in the middle of an open space. Flags waved everywhere.

"This is neat," Jamie said, looking around.

"I've seen this in movies," Alison said with excitement. "Haven't you? Usually, there's skating."

As they walked around, Rodney noticed something. "People are looking at us."

Alison glanced around. Rodney was right. People were

whispering as they walked by. "Do you think they recognize us?"

Her question was answered by a group of giggling ten-year-olds, who came up to them. The smallest of the group pointed and said, "You're Rodney."

"And Luke."

"Wendy." And "Jane."

Amidst the giggles, several managed to find pens and pieces of paper, and they began asking for autographs. One girl, paperless, begged Rodney to sign on her arm.

The boldness of the ten-year-olds inspired other passersby to see who these celebrities were. Then the clamor for autographs really started.

Alison, Jamie, Mike, and Rodney tried to sign as many autographs as they could, but finally Alison whispered, "Phil has probably been around the block ten times by now."

"Right," Jamie said. "Thank you, everybody, but we've got to leave now."

There were some groans, and one woman grabbed Mike's arm, insisting that he sign her newspaper before he left, but finally they escaped, practically running to the limo, which Phil had managed to park illegally.

"Boy, I thought for sure I'd get a ticket. I didn't know there was that much to see in Rockefeller Center."

"Oh, there was something to see," Jamie informed him. "Us."

"You mean people wanted autographs?" Phil asked.

"They sure did," Rodney said happily.

All of the cast members of *Sticks and Stones* had had

people come up to them since the show started, but since they spent so much time at the studio, it had happened only sporadically, and certainly there had never been groups of people like this.

"Maybe we should just go back to the hotel?" Jamie suggested.

"No way," Mike said forcefully. "I want to see New York."

"I want to see if any more girls come up and ask for my autograph," Rodney said.

"Let's just drive by some of these famous places," Alison suggested. "Then we can see stuff and not have to get out of the car."

Since everyone was a little weary from their experience, they all agreed to do the rest of their sightseeing from the back of the limo. Phil drove them past the Empire State Building, then he went over to the East Side so they could see the UN, and finally they wound up in Greenwich Village.

"Is anyone hungry?" Phil called from the front seat.

A chorus of yesses answered him.

"Then I've got a great restaurant for you. And don't worry about privacy," Phil assured them. "I've got an in with the owner."

As it turned out, the tiny restaurant that Phil took them to was owned by his brother, Joe. He greeted all of them like long-lost friends. Phil explained they needed a private room. Joe obligingly took them through the main room, with its gay blue-and-white checked tablecloths, and pictures of famous Italians on the wall, back to a cozy area with brick walls and a swept-out fireplace with a basket of dried flowers in the hearth.

"Oh, this is charming," Alison said.

"You could probably sit in the main room, it's so late in the afternoon," Joe said. "But maybe it will seem more like a party back here."

None of them could ever remember a better party. Deep plates full of fabulous dishes of steaming pastas seemed to appear one after another. There were fabulous salads, and for dessert, tiramisu, which sounded Japanese, but was a special kind of Italian cake.

The meal was difficult for Jamie, but since she hadn't eaten all day, she allowed herself some salad and a few bites of pasta. It tasted heavenly.

The rest of the cast indulged themselves as if they might never eat again.

"This is a wonderful meal," Alison said, turning to Joe with eyes shining.

Joe nodded. "Welcome to New York."

Chapter 7

"So how was your shopping trip?" Jamie asked from her bed, where she was snuggled under the covers reading a book.

Alison held up a couple of shopping bags. "It's a good thing the stores were open until nine. I neeeded everything from underwear to barrettes. I don't suppose my luggage has shown up?"

"Why do you care? You got tons of new stuff."

"I know, I know." Alison began hanging up her new clothes. "But I *had* to get something. We're going to be on the *Today* show tomorrow."

"I could hardly forget."

"Are you nervous?" Alison asked.

Jamie nodded. Even she had to admit she was a little apprehensive about this one.

"Mike and Rodney are going to be on one of those afternoon talk shows with some grown-up kid stars."

"At least we'll only have a couple of minutes of air

time," Jamie said. "Poor Mike and Rodney will be sitting under those hot lights for an hour."

Alison sighed. "Yeah, but the day after tomorrow, we've got that local talk show, and from what Cindy said we're going to be the whole show."

"So?" Jamie asked with a shrug. "After being on the *Today* show, everything else will seem like small potatoes."

Alison started undressing. *Jamie just doesn't understand,* she thought to herself. *I'm on the verge of totally losing it.* If she let herself think about doing the shows for longer than a few minutes, her head started pounding, her stomach churned, and her palms began to sweat. After she took off her makeup and got into her pajamas, Alison crawled into bed. Jamie said good night and turned off the light, but after about ten minutes Alison said, "I suppose this is futile."

"What do you mean?"

"I'm exhausted, but I'm not sleepy. Does that make any sense?"

"I've been there. Maybe you should try a glass of warm milk," Jamie suggested.

"Do we have milk up here?" Alison asked, confused.

"Think room service."

Alison was embarrassed but called down for a glass of milk, which was brought up on a small silver tray. It didn't work. There was no point in keeping Jamie up too, so Alison did her pacing in the living room.

I'm going to be a wreck tomorrow morning, and Cindy wasn't all that thrilled with the way I looked this morning.

That thought woke her up even more. Alison stopped her pacing to stare out the window, but instead of marveling at at the lovely view of Manhattan, Alison could only wonder how many of the residents asleep in all those apartments watched the *Today* show.

This isn't doing any good, she told herself, and picked up a book she had brought with her. Reading was supposed to make a person sleepy, but Alison read until almost three-thirty.

The wake-up call came even earlier the next morning than the day before. Jamie rolled over and asked Alison, "Do you mind if I take my shower first?"

There was barely a groan from Alison, so Jamie got up and hit the shower. She had assumed that by the time she was done in the bathroom, Alison would at least be up and about, but she was still in bed, snoring lightly.

Jamie started to get dressed, glancing over her shoulder at Alison every few minutes. She knew she should wake Alison up; time was running short. But a part of her just wanted to let Alison sleep. Sleep and miss the interview entirely.

It was a horrible thought, and Jamie felt guilty even thinking it. Besides, she could never get away with it. What would Cindy say if she waltzed downstairs without Alison? She'd hardly believe that Jamie hadn't noticed that her roommate was still asleep.

No, going on the *Today* show without Alison was a nice fantasy, but it was just that, a fantasy.

"Hey, sleepyhead," Jamie said, going over and giving Alison a shake. "Get up."

"Hmmm," Alison mumbled, and tried to turn over.

"No, no you don't," Jamie said, pulling down her covers. "You've got to get up."

Alison opened her blue eyes and looked at Jamie blankly.

"The *Today* show? Remember?"

Alison jumped out of bed. "Oh my gosh. I'm late."

"Well, you're getting there."

"Why didn't you wake me?" Alison cried.

"You heard the wake-up call. I thought you'd be up when I came out of the bathroom."

Alison hurried into the bathroom and slammed the door.

As Jamie leisurely continued getting ready, she realized that things were working out pretty well. Alison was awfully flustered about oversleeping. That wouldn't help her performance this morning.

"Alison, I'm going downstairs," Jamie called. "I'll tell Cindy you're right behind me."

Alison stuck her head out of the bathroom, a panicked look on her face. "But I'm not ready," she wailed.

"You've got a few minutes. I just don't think we should both keep Cindy waiting."

Alison nodded and slammed the door. "I'll be down as soon as I can," came her muffled reply.

Cindy was already waiting in the limo when Jamie joined her.

"Where's Alison?" Cindy asked with a frown.

"She's still getting ready."

"I suppose we've got a little time." Cindy settled back in her seat. "Are you nervous?" she asked.

Jamie nodded. "Who wouldn't be?"

"I heard you did a great job on the radio interview. Unlike Alison." Cindy was frowning again.

"Thank you," was all that Jamie said. She didn't want to seem like she was gloating. But maybe, just maybe, there was something that she did better than Alison.

"I can't believe I screwed up again," Alison moaned.

"Come on, Alison," Jamie insisted. "You weren't that bad."

Alison just looked at her.

Jamie didn't know what to say. It was true. Alison had been awful.

When they arrived at the studio, they had been whisked into makeup and Alison had actually seemed calm. But as soon as they were under the lights, being introduced to Katie Couric, Jamie had looked over and noticed that Alison was shaking a little.

Katie noticed, too, and tried to put Alison at her ease. "This will be over before you know it," she said with a smile.

Alison nodded, but it didn't seem to calm her down any.

"Okay, ten seconds to air time," the assistant director called to them.

As soon as she was cued, Katie introduced Alison and Jamie to the audience. Then she showed a brief clip of them on *Sticks and Stones*. When they came back live, Katie turned to Jamie first and asked her why she thought the show was such an instant hit.

"Well, I'd like to say it was Alison and me," Jamie said

in a deprecating tone, "but I think it's a whole lot more. We've got a terrific cast, especially our veterans Ben Epson and Donna Wheeler. And the writers are great. Every week we have really funny scripts."

Katie turned to Alison. "Alison, this is your first job, right?"

It was a rerun of the radio show. About all Alison could do was nod, leaving it to Jamie to tell the whole story about how she got the job. Whenever Katie asked Alison a question, she managed a one-word answer, leaving Jamie to amplify on it. It was over quicker than she would have hoped, but that didn't make her terrible performance any easier to take.

Am I being too hard on myself? Alison had wondered on the ride back to the hotel. Apparently not. Cindy had complimented Jamie on her performance, making her lack of comment to Alison all the more obvious. When they got back to the hotel, Cindy had pulled her aside and said, "I'm going to look into finding a coach or someone who can prep you."

Once Jamie and Alison were back in the suite, Jamie watched as Alison flopped herself down on bed, her head toward the wall. Though Jamie had wanted Alison to fail, now, with Alison looking so dejected, it was hard to gloat. Jamie had been humiliated enough in her own life to know it was a horrible feeling.

She tried to think of something that would make Alison feel better. "Why don't we just forget about the silly *Today* show? We've got a whole day ahead of us. We could go to a museum or shop . . ."

"I don't think so," Alison said, barely raising her head.

"Well, what would you like to do?" Jamie asked.

"I think I'd just like to go to sleep."

"Now?"

"I didn't get much sleep last night." Alison sat up. "Of course, I could have gotten eight hours of uninterrupted sleep, and still not have been able to say a word."

Jamie didn't know what to say.

"I wish I could call my parents," Alison said quietly.

"So why don't you?"

"They're in the middle of the ocean."

"That's right, the cruise."

Alison could feel tears forming in her eyes. She would hate crying in front of Jamie, so she blinked them back furiously.

A knock at the door gave Alison the opportunity to get away from Jamie's pitying gaze. She got up and let in the bellboy. He had a big smile on his face.

"Your luggage," he said, holding up her bags.

"Oh, thank you," Alison said, a real smile crossing her face for the first time all day. "Where were they?"

"At the wrong hotel, apparently," the bellboy said, bringing the bags inside. "Shall I put them in the bedroom?"

"Please."

"Your bags," Jamie said happily. "See, Alison, things are looking up."

Alison fished some money out of her purse and tipped the bellboy. "I've got a way to go on that score," she replied.

Once they were alone, Alison opened her suitcase. Tippy was stuffed into one side, and Alison pulled him out. "You're a little late, good-luck charm," she told him.

"Maybe the good luck is just about to start," Jamie suggested. *Boy you sound like a Pollyanna,* she told herself.

Alison nodded, but Jamie could tell she didn't believe a word.

"Do you mind if I go to a museum?" Jamie asked. "I mean, I'll stay with you if you like . . ."

"And watch me sleep? Of course, that might be less painful than watching me on television. Or listening to me on the radio."

"Come on, Alison. Don't beat yourself up. Look, I'm going to stay."

"No," Alison insisted. "Don't be silly. I really do want to catch a nap."

"And you'll probably sleep better if I'm not here. All right, then, I'll go." Jamie picked up her purse. "Now, remember, we've got that dinner with the sponsors and their advertising agency tonight."

"Don't look so worried," Alison said. "As far as I know, I'm still capable of talking to people around a dinner table." Alison's tone was bold, but at this moment she wondered if what she had said was true.

Alone at last in her room, Alison crawled under the covers and hugged Tippy to her. Disappointment and exhaustion finally overwhelmed her and Alison burst into tears. Everything up until this trip had been golden. She couldn't believe how quickly it had tarnished.

As she rode down in the elevator, Jamie tried to decide if

she should go to the Museum of Modern Art or the Metropolitan Museum. The Met was such an impressive building, and Jamie knew their collection was one of the finest in the world, but the avant-garde paintings and sculpture at the Museum of Modern Art were really more her style.

The doors to the ornate lobby opened, and Jamie hurried out. She thought she might ask the concierge if there were any special exhibits on at either museum. She wasn't paying any attention to the people around her, so she jumped with surprise when she felt someone grab her arm.

"Oh, Mike," Jamie said with relief. "You scared me."

"Sorry. I just wanted to ask how it went this morning."

Jamie led him over to an overstuffed couch. "Not great."

"Alison screwed up?" he asked with concern.

Jamie nodded. "Big time. She barely said a word."

"And how did you feel when Alison screwed up live on national television?"

Jamie felt as if Mike was looking right inside her, knowing exactly what she had been thinking that morning when she let Alison sleep. But she certainly wasn't going to confirm Mike's suspicions. "What do you mean by that?" she asked indignantly.

"Jamie, it's no secret why Alison suddenly reinterpreted her role at our first dress rehearsal. *You* coached her."

"That's right, it's no secret. What's the big deal? It worked out, didn't it?" Jamie asked carefully.

"Yeah, but it could just as easily have been a big fiasco," Mike said, his eyes fixed on her.

He suspects I tried to get Alison fired, Jamie thought.

Jamie summoned all her acting experience to convince Mike he was wrong. "Unlike you, Mike, I've been on a television show. I know that producers and directors like it if an actress does a little more with a role than read her lines. I told Alison that, sure. But I was only trying to help."

Mike continued to stare at her for a few minutes, then looked away. "I'd like to think so."

Jamie decided the best defense was a good offense. "I hope you're not going to cause trouble, Mike."

Shrugging, he said, "I'm not going to do anything that makes it worse for Alison."

"Look, I'm going to the museum. If you're through with your insinuations, I think I'll get going."

"Don't let me stop you."

Jamie was about to walk away when Cindy came up to them.

"We need to have a short meeting tomorrow afternoon about the American Choice Awards," she informed them.

"Are we going to rehearse the thing?" Mike wanted to know.

"Yes. The show will be sending over the particulars tomorrow, so we can go over it as soon as you come back from that talk show. I've already told Rodney's mother to alert him."

"Will you let Alison know, or should I?" Jamie asked. "She's upstairs sleeping now."

"I'm not sure Alison is going to be on the show," Cindy said slowly.

"You're kidding," Mike said with surprise.

"I thought it was going to be all four of us," Jamie added.

"Look," Cindy said bluntly, "you know she's bombed out on every live interview we've sent her on. I can't have her screwing up another national television show. Especially one in prime time."

"But those were talk shows," Mike protested. "She'll have lines she can memorize for the awards show."

"She can't sleep, she looks bad, and she obviously can't talk. Right now Alison is so rattled, I can't count on her to perform on any live TV show."

"But she'll die if she can't do it," Jamie said, honestly upset for Alison. "She'll be totally humiliated."

"Better Alison humiliated in private than *Sticks and Stones* in public. We'll just say she's taken ill." Cindy's voice softened a little as she read the upset looks on their faces. "Sorry, guys. That's show business."

Chapter 8

Jamie and Mike exchanged glances. Cindy was serious, and they knew it.

I should be loving this, Jamie thought. *Mike probably thinks I am loving it.* But all Jamie could do was feel worried about Alison.

Only yesterday Alison had been chattering about the awards show, wondering if the evening gown she had worn for the photo shoot would be a good choice or if she should look for something else. Then, with Jamie's help, she had tried out several different hairdos, piling her hair up on top of her head and then twisting it into a French roll. Alison had seemed totally into it, really excited.

If Cindy didn't let Alison be a presenter, Jamie knew that it would undermine any confidence she had left. Mike tried to make that point to Cindy.

"If you cancel Alison," Mike warned, "I'm not sure she'll get over it."

"It could affect her work on *Sticks and Stones,*" Jamie added. "You wouldn't want that would you?"

Cindy grimaced. "I realize it's a gamble, and of course I'll discuss this with Dan before I make any final decisions, but remember, if Alison screws up on the awards show, that's not going to boost her confidence either."

"When do you have to decide?" Mike wanted to know.

"Well, I should probably let the American Choice people know sometime today. If Alison's not going to appear, I have to give the producers plenty of notice."

"Maybe you can hold off until after tomorrow's talk show," Jamie pleaded.

Cindy shook her head. "That's awfully late."

"But maybe Alison will do a great job," Jamie argued.

"I don't know," Cindy said, looking doubtful. "Maybe I should pull her off tomorrow's show, too."

This is getting worse and worse, Jamie thought.

"Alison can turn it all around," Mike said forcefully. "I know she can."

"And exactly what would make that happen?" Cindy asked simply.

Jamie and Mike looked at each other.

"I'm not sure," Jamie finally said honestly, "but maybe Mike and I can come up with a way to help."

"She at least deserves one more chance on live TV," Mike added. "That's not asking so much."

"All right," Cindy said with a sigh. "But I've got to talk to Dan about it today. If he agrees, I'll try to find a coach and we'll see how she does with tomorrow's interview before I say anything about the awards show."

Cindy left Jamie and Mike standing in the lobby wondering just what they could do to help.

"Maybe I can talk to her," Mike said slowly.

"Wait until she wakes up, she needs her sleep. And you can't say anything to upset her," Jamie warned him.

"I know, I know. I'll just have to figure out the right thing to say."

"And I'll try to come up with a plan, too."

Mike looked at her curiously. "Can it be I had you wrong, Jamie?"

Jamie didn't answer that. Let Mike think whatever he wanted. "I'm going to the museum. I'll let you know if I've had any ideas when I get back."

A half an hour later, Jamie was wandering around the Museum of Modern Art, trying to enjoy the pictures, but her mind was back in the hotel.

Mike's comments also kept rolling around in her head. She was surprised that Mike had figured out her ploy to get Alison fired. She was even more surprised at her own reaction to the news that Alison was finally doing something wrong for a change.

Why, she wondered, was her first instinct to help Alison? Only earlier today she had been tempted to let Alison sleep through her interview. Yet one thing she was sure of, when Cindy said Alison was off the awards show, Jamie knew she didn't want that to happen. Maybe she wasn't as hardhearted as she thought.

Jamie decided that trying to wander around the museum any further was silly. She had noticed a nice little coffee shop down the street. Perhaps she would just go there, sit down, and try to sort out all these confusing thoughts.

The streets were crowded. It seemed everyone in New

York walked, unlike in Los Angeles, where most people drove everywhere. Why, there were certain elite parts of Los Angeles where the police would question pedestrians because walking was so unusual. Jamie looked around and decided she liked this better. There was an energy in the air that was missing in L.A.

She found the coffee shop and went inside. She chose a back table and ordered a cappuccino.

So what's with this great sympathy for Alison? she asked herself as she waited for her order to come. *Alison's great fiasco should have gladdened my heart. If everything worked out the way it seemed it was going to, Alison would be so upset, she'd start blowing her lines on* Sticks and Stones *and then she'd be off just like I wished from day one.*

But watching Alison these last few days, Jamie had realized just how vulnerable Alison was. She wasn't the rich girl paper doll that Jamie had always assumed. Alison was a living, breathing kid, full of insecurities just like she was. And even all her parents' money couldn't help her when she screwed up big time.

Jamie sipped the cappuccino that the waitress put down in front of her. It was time to be honest with herself. What had Alison ever done to her but try to be a friend? Well, maybe the time had come to return the favor. But how?

"Excuse me?"

Jamie looked up to see a girl about her own age with wire-rimmed glasses standing in front of her.

"Yes?"

The girl cleared her throat. "You're on *Sticks and Stones.* You're Jamie O'Leary, aren't you?"

"That's right."

"Can I sit down for a minute?" the girl asked shyly.

Jamie didn't want to be bothered, but the girl looked so hopeful, Jamie felt it would be rude to just send her away. "Sure, have a seat. Your name is . . . ?"

"Iris."

"Have a seat, Iris."

"I won't stay long," Iris said gratefully. "I just had to tell you how much I like you. And your show."

"Thanks." It was fun to get compliments like this.

"I watch it every week. I never miss it."

Jamie felt herself being warmed by the girl's enthusiasm.

"And I think I know why the show is such a big hit," Iris told her.

"Really? Why?"

"I think it's the way you all are with each other."

"What do you mean?" Jamie asked, curious.

"You don't always get along on the show, but you make it interesting and real. I have a stepsister of my own, so I know."

"Most of that is the writing," Jamie said, a little embarrassed. "We have really good writers."

Iris shook her head. "It's not just that the show is funny. It's that you make it so much fun. Even when you're not getting along."

"I guess we do," Jamie said thoughtfully. It was true, the way they all worked together was the most important part of the show.

"Could I have an autograph?" Iris asked.

Jamie refocused on Iris. "Oh, of course."

Iris fumbled around in her bag and pulled out a piece of paper and a pen, and Jamie scribbled her name.

"I should let you drink your coffee," Iris said, looking shy once more.

Jumping up, Jamie said, "No. I'm done. I mean, I just had an idea, and I've got to get on it."

Iris looked confused. "An idea? Was it something I said?"

Jamie flashed a bright smile at her. "It sure was. Thanks." She grabbed her purse and hurried out of the restaurant. Maybe there was a way to help Alison after all.

"Oh, hi, Mike," Alison said, opening the door to her suite. She was a little embarrassed to have him see her like this, sleepy-eyed, her hair a mess, but she couldn't just send him away. "I was taking a nap." She giggled nervously. "But you probably guessed that."

"I could go . . ."

"No." Alison opened the door wider. "Come in."

"Jamie's not back yet?" he asked, coming into the room.

Alison shrugged. "I guess not." She looked down at her T-shirt and shorts. They were so wrinkled. Here was Mike, come to call, and she looked like she had just rolled out of bed, which of course she had.

"What time is it?" she asked.

"About four."

Alison sat down on the couch, and Mike sat next to her. "Four o'clock!" Alison said, waking up a little. "You've already done your talk show. How did it go?"

Mike had no intention of telling Alison it went great. That he and Rodney had broken up the audience with laughter and that the host had told them they ought to have their own show. "It went all right, I guess."

"Did you see me on the *Today* show?" Alison asked quietly.

Mike had known that Alison was going to ask that question and up until this very second he wasn't sure how he would answer. He looked at Alison's sad, dejected face, and even though he wanted to lie up a storm, he said, "I didn't see it. But I heard it wasn't so hot."

"Terrible," Alison murmured.

"You can make it up," Mike said forcefully.

"Yeah, right."

"You have another chance."

Alison gave him a trembly smile. "Oh, has the *Today* show asked me back for a repeat performance?"

"No. But we all are going on that talk show tomorrow, *New York A.M.*"

"Another chance for me to sit on television like a statue."

"Another chance for you to show people what a terrific, funny girl you are."

Alison got up and started pacing the floor. "I can't do it, Mike. Haven't I proven that?"

"So you've had a couple of bad experiences. What do they say about falling off a horse? You have to get right back on and try again."

"I've fallen twice. I'm sore."

Patting the seat on the couch next to him, Mike said,

"Stop wearing out the carpet, Ali. Come over and sit down."

Alison was taken aback by the use of her nickname. Only her family and closest friends called her Ali. She did as Mike asked and sat down next to him.

Had she ever been this close to him? she wondered. Close enough to smell his cologne?

Mike put his arm around Alison, and she could feel herself shiver a little.

"Are you cold?" Mike asked.

"No." Then she wondered if she should have said yes. At least it would have been an excuse.

But Mike didn't seem to think anything of her answer. All he said was, "You can do a good job on that show tomorrow. I know you can."

"I don't know what comes over me," Alison said plaintively. "I just start wondering what the next question will be and how will I answer. Then my mind goes blank."

Mike pulled her a little closer. "We'll figure it out," he said.

For a few wild seconds, Alison was actually glad that she was screwing up so badly. Who cared, if it meant sitting here with Mike's arm around her?

Was he going to kiss her? He was leaning very close. Then the sound of a key in the door made him remove his arm quickly.

"Hi," Jamie said brightly as she walked into the living room. *Uh-oh,* she thought. *What have I interrupted?* There were some very strange vibes flying around the room.

Alison jumped up. "How was the museum? Do you

want something to drink? I can get it out of the minibar.''

"The museum was fine. And I just had some coffee, so no thanks.''

"We should probably start getting ready for the dinner.''

Jamie glanced at her watch. "Yes. We've got to be downstairs in about an hour.''

"Do you mind if I take a shower first?'' Alison asked.

Jamie flopped down on a chair. "Not at all. I want to rest for a few minutes anyway.''

"Okay.'' Alison turned to Mike. "Thanks for the kind words.'' But she didn't look much happier.

"What did you say?'' Jamie asked, as soon as Alison was out of earshot.

"I just tried to encourage her, tell her she could do it. Frankly, I couldn't think of anything else.''

"Well, that's all right,'' Jamie said with satisfaction. "Because I have.''

Mike leaned forward. "You're kidding.''

"Nope,'' Jamie said, shaking her head. "It just came to me, and I think it will work.''

"So let's hear it.''

"After I went to the museum, I stopped in a coffee shop. A fan named Iris came up to me, and she said she knew what made the show so good.''

"I've been kind of wondering that myself.''

"She said it was the way we all worked together. The way we all played off each other.''

"I guess that's true,'' Mike said slowly. "But what does that have to do with helping Alison?''

"That's just it. We haven't been helping Alison. Not even people like Dan and Cindy."

"You've been on the air with her every time she messed up," Mike pointed out.

"Yes, and I thought all I had to do was jump in whenever there was a lull in the conversation. That may have kept the show moving, but obviously it hasn't done much for Alison."

Mike looked at her skeptically. "And you didn't get a charge out of it all? It didn't help your ego just a little showing up Alison?"

Jamie wished that Mike didn't understand her quite so perfectly, but there was no point in lying anymore. "Of course I liked it. I admit it," she said almost defiantly. "It made me feel good that I was the golden girl for a change."

"That's what I thought," Mike said triumphantly.

"So are you going to sit there and gloat, or are you going to listen to my plan?"

That stopped Mike. "Listen. *If* you're really sincere about helping Alison."

"I'm getting a little tired of having to defend myself, Mike. What do you want me to do? Get down on my hands and knees?"

"All right," Mike said, looking contrite. "I'm sorry too. I shouldn't be ragging you."

"Thank you."

"Now, what can we do for Ali?"

Jamie noted the nickname, but decided to let it pass. "If we were getting a new script for the show, we'd all be working together to learn the lines."

"So?"

"So," Jamie said impatiently, "we go about this talk show like it's a script. We all sit down with Alison, practice the questions we know these interviewers are going to ask, and rehearse the answers. By the time we're done with Alison, she'll be word perfect."

Mike looked at Jamie with admiration. Probably the first time he ever had, Jamie thought.

"I think you've got something there, Jamie."

"Told you."

"If Alison feels comfortable with the answers, she won't worry, and she'll do just fine."

"I think we should get Rodney in on this too," Jamie said, enthusiastically planning. "Alison likes him a lot and he lightens everything up."

"That's a good idea."

"What's a good idea?" Alison asked, coming out of the shower in a robe with a towel wrapped around her head.

"Alison Blake," Mike announced with a smile. "You're about to become the queen of talk shows."

Chapter 9

Alison didn't know whether to laugh or cry. "That's me all right, a regular Oprah."

Mike and Jamie exchanged glances. Obviously this was going to take some work.

Mike cleared his throat. "Jamie has come up with a pretty good strategy."

"Pretty good!" Jamie said with indignation. "Great."

"Okay, great," Mike said agreeably.

"What are you going to do? Hire a ventriloquist to stand behind me and answer my questions?"

"Very funny," Mike said. "No. We are going to rehearse this talk show until you're word perfect."

Constantly interrupting each other, Jamie and Mike filled Alison in.

At first, it all seemed like a stupid, hopeless dream. "How are you going to figure out what questions they'll ask?" Alison demanded. "They could come up with anything."

"Not really," Jamie said. "Think about it. They always ask about how you got the job and why the show is so popular."

Mike nodded. "That's the sort of stuff I'm getting, too."

"But there's always something new," Alison protested.

"There's not a question those talk-show hosts can think of that we won't think of first," Mike promised.

For the first time, Alison looked hopeful. "It might work."

"It *will* work," Jamie said firmly. "We'll get on it tomorrow morning."

"Hey, we can even practice tonight," Mike improvised.

"Tonight?" Alison asked. Even Jamie looked surprised.

"When we're at the dinner. You don't have trouble just making conversation, do you?"

"No," Alison replied indignantly. Did Mike think she was a total idiot?

"So, pretend there's a camera watching you tonight. Pretend all the chitchat is happening on a talk show."

"Good thought, Mike," Jamie said approvingly. "That's the effect these shows are going for anyway. Casual. As if the hosts are meeting their guests across a dinner table."

"I guess it might work," Alison said slowly. "Of course, there's always the chance I'll imagine TV cameras, and I'll sit there stuffing rolls in my mouth, not saying a word."

"I won't pass you the rolls." Mike said.

That made Alison laugh.

"I'm going to take a bath," Jamie said. She got up and patted Alison on the shoulder. "Don't worry anymore. This is going to work."

Once they were alone, Alison turned to Mike. "I guess you'd better get ready, too."

"Are you feeling better?"

Alison thought about it for a second. "Yes. Yes, I am."

"Well, that's a first step."

Mike got up and Alison walked him to the door. "Mike?"

"Yes?"

"Thank you."

"It was really Jamie's idea. She's the one you ought to thank."

Alison wasn't sure how to say what she wanted to. It was great that Jamie had come up with a way to help her, but it was Mike she wanted to be proud of her. "You helped a lot," she finally said.

Mike took Alison's face very gently in his hands and pulled her close. Then, very lightly, he kissed her. Without saying another word, he was gone.

Alison stood there, staring at the door. The kiss was so swift, she wondered if it had actually happened. Yes, it had. Mike had kissed her, and it was the sweetest kiss she'd ever received.

The dinner went better than Alison expected. She was seated next to a very nice man who reminded her of her father. Stanley Evans was president of the soft drink company that bought a lot of commercials on *Sticks and Stones*.

Alison did what Jamie and Mike suggested. She pretended that cameras were set up around the lovely private room in the French restaurant Cindy had chosen for the dinner. But she didn't remember the cameras for very long. Mr. Evans loved to talk and was easy to talk to. Before long, she was conversing in an easy, natural manner.

Jamie, on the other hand, was having a most uncomfortable evening. She was sitting between the head of the advertising agency and another sponsor's wife. Both of them liked their food, and they spent most of the dinner *ooh*ing and *aah*ing over the various courses.

"This mushroom mousse is to die for!" Mrs. Lester said, daintily dabbing her lips.

"Excellent," Mr. Dennis agreed.

Mrs. Lester looked at Jamie's plate. "You haven't touched your mousse."

"I . . . I don't care for mushrooms."

"You're really missing a treat," Mrs. Lester said.

"But the rack of lamb is on the way," Mr. Dennis informed her. "I'm sure you'll enjoy that."

Jamie could feel her stomach tighten. The thought of shoveling down a whole rack of lamb made her queasy. But what was she going to do? She couldn't very well say she didn't like lamb, either.

When the entrée arrived, complete with tiny new potatoes and asparagus, Jamie cut it into the tiniest pieces she could and slowly ate several of them. She could feel Mrs. Lester and Mr. Dennis giving her sidelong glances.

"How's the lamb?" Mr. Dennis asked.

"Delicious."

"You're only nibbling at it," Mrs. Lester noted.

"I had a big lunch."

"You're entirely too thin, dear," Mrs. Lester continued as if Jamie hadn't spoken. "You're not on one of those crazy diets, are you?"

"No." Jamie's tone was little sharper than she meant it to be. She had to remember these people were important. "It's just that you have to be so careful when you're on television," she tried to explain more nicely. "The cameras always add weight."

"Just don't let it go too far," Mr. Dennis advised. "You don't want to look like a skeleton." Mr. Dennis took another hearty bite of his lamb.

"I won't." Jamie felt obligated to heap her fork with food and try to smile while she ate.

By the time Jamie got back to the hotel, she was in a very bad mood. All her good feelings about helping Alison seemed to have dissipated. Now she was tired and depressed. The one thing she wasn't, was hungry.

Alison hadn't come back yet. She and Mike had decided to skip the limo and walk because it was such a nice night.

Throwing her dress on the floor of the bedroom, Jamie wondered what was going on between those two. How could there suddenly be this big romance? Only a couple of days ago, Alison seemed like a shy little rabbit whenever Mike was around.

Oh well, Jamie thought, *I never had a chance with Mike anyway.* If Alison thought she could keep up with Mike, let her.

Jamie knew she was feeling grumpy because of the dinner. The best thing to do was to just go to bed. There was a lot to accomplish tomorrow with Alison.

She thought about taking a nice, relaxing bath, but she had just had one earlier in the evening. Brushing her teeth, Jamie decided she'd just get into bed and read until she fell asleep. If she could sleep after all she had eaten.

So I might turn into a skeleton, Jamie thought bitterly, Mr. Dennis's words floating back at her.

She examined herself in the full-length mirror on the door. "I'm hardly a skeleton," Jamie said aloud. She pinched a roll of fat around her stomach. True, there wasn't as much there as before, but she could grab enough to shake.

When would the day come when there wouldn't be any fat at all? she wondered, giving her tummy an extra-vicious tug.

She was so tempted to use one of the methods Pierce had talked about for getting rid of some of this excess food. Would it be all that difficult to make herself throw up?

She shuddered as she turned away from the mirror. That was so utterly gross. She'd just have to continue her dieting and understand that every once in a while she was going to fall, or be forced to fall, off the dieting wagon. Tomorrow she'd just try harder, eat less. Usually that thought cheered her. Tonight, it just made her feel sad.

Alison was already awake and bouncing around the room when Jamie awakened the next morning. "What's with you?" Jamie said, rubbing her eyes.

Despite her new, friendly feelings for Jamie, Alison didn't feel like confiding. Last night was so special, so personal, that she wanted to hold all those wonderful feelings close.

Cindy had looked a little skeptical when she and Mike said they wanted to walk home. ''Do you think that's a good idea?''

''Cindy,'' Mike said, with a crooked grin, ''we're going to walk down Fifth Avenue, one of the busiest streets in the city, at dusk. I don't think much can happen to us. Do you?''

When Mike put it like that, Cindy couldn't very well object. What Mike had failed to mention was that he had other plans besides just walking home. When they reached Central Park, across the street from their hotel, he pointed to the shiny black horse-drawn carriages that waited to take people on romantic moonlit rides through the park.

''What do you say we go for a ride?''

Alison had been longing to go ever since their arrival in New York, but she had never imagined she might actually go with Mike.

''Oh, yes, let's,'' she said with eyes shining.

They had ridden around the park with Alison snuggled against Mike. The one little kiss in the hotel had multiplied into stronger, more passionate kisses. Unlike so many times with Brad, when it had been Alison who called a halt, now it was Mike who eased away.

''Ali, we've got to slow down.''

Alison came out of her trance enough to nod.

''I don't want to rush anything with you,'' Mike said seriously.

She straightened up and began babbling. ''I know. And it's so complicated, us working together and all.''

"It's not about work," Mike said seriously. "It's about us taking our time."

Mike had seemed so protective. So warm. Alison knew this was one night she was never going to forget.

"Mike thought we should meet here this morning since we're in the suite," Alison said.

"Fine," Jamie said getting out of bed. "Maybe you should order some rolls and coffee."

By the time Jamie was dressed, the food had arrived and so had Cindy. Luckily, Alison was now in the shower, so Jamie had a chance to explain the plan to her.

Cindy flopped down on the couch. "Well, I suppose we have to give it a chance. I had a coach all lined up for this morning and she phoned in sick. So now you guys are all we've got."

"Did you talk to Dan?"

"No. I couldn't reach him last night, but he's supposed to call me this morning."

Alison walked into the living room. "I guess you're talking about me, huh?"

Cindy nodded. "Tell me honestly, Alison, do you want to do this talk show? I can get you off it." She didn't say anything about the awards show.

"I think this idea of Jamie's is going to work," Alison said simply.

Cindy searched her face. "Well, you certainly look better. Did you try some new makeup?"

Alison didn't want to tell Cindy that her glow came from her evening with Mike. "I just got a good night's sleep."

"Well, that's a start," Cindy said with a sigh. She didn't look too happy when she left the suite.

"She doesn't buy it," Alison said, turning to Jamie.

Jamie shrugged. "So we prove her wrong."

"Or right," Alison muttered.

Alison's rapidly souring mood was interrupted by the arrival of Mike and Rodney. Rodney was very excited; practically rubbing his hands in glee over his role in remaking Alison.

"I feel like Henry Higgens in *My Fair Lady*," Rodney informed the girls.

"Whoa," Alison said. "I don't need you guys to make me over. Just make me coherent on talk shows."

"And that's just what we're going to do," Mike agreed. "Now why don't we sit like we're on a talk show. I'll play the host."

Alison felt a little silly, but she settled herself on the couch between Jamie and Rodney.

"Now, Alison," Mike said in the sugary voice of a talk-show host. "Tell the audience. How did you get discovered for your new hit show, *Sticks and Stones?*"

Two hours later, when the group had decided they could quit with confidence, Alison was word perfect in her answers. She could tell with ease the story of how she was found in the waiting room. She could comment on the scripts, the audience, even on the show that came on before *Sticks and Stones*. Jamie had been right. Learning the answers as if they were lines in a script did make her feel as if she could handle the whole thing. At least she felt that way here, safe in this hotel suite. She hoped it would translate once she got back into a television studio.

"Hey, Alison," Rodney said, "what do you think of your co-stars?"

Alison giggled. "How many times do you want me to go over that one?"

"Just let's hear what you think of me."

"Rodney is precocious and great to work with," Alison chanted. "You never know what he's going to do next."

"I know what he's going to do next," Mike said. "Get off his duff and get ready for this interview."

Cindy came down from her room to remind them of the same thing. "So how did it go?" she asked.

"I think it helped," Alison bubbled.

"Alison is word perfect," Rodney informed Cindy.

"Really?"

"Just watch and find out," Jamie said confidently.

Even wary Cindy looked hopeful.

The kids got their coats and headed out to the limo. As they walked through the lobby, Cindy pulled Mike aside.

"I talked to Dan. He was very concerned about Alison's performances on the talk shows and he agrees with me that if she messes up today we'll have to keep her off the awards show."

"But if she's okay, there's no problem, right?" Mike asked anxiously.

Cindy nodded. "For what it's worth, I think you guys have done a terrific thing, no matter how it turns out."

The studio was located in the heart of midtown Manhattan. A perky young woman, Jenny Thomas, the show's host, came into the Green Room, where all the guests sat, to say hello.

"The whole show is going to be devoted to the cast of *Sticks and Stones,*" Jenny informed them. "First I'll talk to you, then we'll have the audience jump in."

Alison looked at her castmates in panic. It was one thing to figure out what a professional talk-show host would ask her. But who knew what fans calling in might say?

As soon as Jenny left the room, everyone turned to Alison.

"Don't worry," Rodney said. "I'll handle the audience."

Even Alison had to laugh at that. "I don't think that will be necessary."

"There are only so many questions in the world, Alison," Jamie said dryly. "I think we quizzed you on ninety percent of them, so it's pretty unlikely the other ten will come up."

"And even if they do," Mike said, "by the time we get around to the audience, you'll be so comfortable you'll handle anything."

Alison could feel tears welling up in her eyes.

"Come on, now," Jamie said sharply. "Don't lose it before we even start."

"That's not why I'm crying," Alison said, wiping away a single fallen tear.

"Then why?" Rodney asked.

"You're all so great. You really care about me. No matter how this turns out, I can't tell you what your help means to me."

In a few minutes, they were led out to the set. It was supposed to look like someone's living room, but as in all television, the set was only illusion. The freestanding fireplace wasn't connected to anything and all the healthy looking plants that decorated the set were fakes.

Jenny seated them around a large oak table. "Are you ready?" she asked them.

All heads involuntarily toward Alison. "Yes," she said, answering for all of them.

Was she ready? She could feel the same nervous energy coursing through her, but she also knew she had some ammunition to fight the scared feelings.

The show started in almost the exact same way as the others had. Jenny introduced the whole cast and showed a clip from the show. As soon as she came back, she turned to Alison. "I hear there's a very funny story about how you got cast on the show."

Alison flashed her friends a grin. If there was one anecdote she had down pat, it was this one. She told the whole story, accentuating the most amusing parts, like how important it was that she had red hair. It really was like acting a part she had rehearsed.

As soon as she was finished, Jenny turned to Jamie and wanted to know about her days on *The Happydale Girls*, giving Alison a breather. Alison immediately glanced at Mike, who discreetly gave her the thumbs-up sign.

After a question for Mike, and one for Rodney about being the youngest kid on the show, Jenny turned to Alison again. "Is there any rivalry between you and Jamie?"

That was one question they hadn't rehearsed, and Alison

could feel the familiar sensation of not knowing what to say come over her. Jamie, sitting next to her, gave her a slight kick, which served to refocus Alison. Then Jamie tossed her hair.

Alison got the hint. "Well, we are both redheads, so there can be fireworks on the show," Alison responded. Then her voice softened. "But I can't tell you how much I've learned from Jamie."

Jamie put her arm around Alison and gave her a little squeeze. "Thanks."

The rest of the show went swimmingly. There was only time for a couple of questions from the audience. A woman from New Jersey wanted to know if Mike was romantically involved with anyone.

Alison, who hoped she wasn't blushing, was as interested in the answer as the woman from New Jersey.

"I'm working on it," was Mike's only answer.

The last question was for Alison from a teenager in the audience. "Your whole life got switched around in a second, wasn't it weird?"

"Weirder than you can ever know."

Chapter 10

"There's Candice Bergen!" Alison poked Jamie in the arm, hard.

"No! Where?"

"Darn, she just went around that corner. But maybe we'll see her later." Alison sat down on a folding chair, one of the several backstage at the American Choice Awards rehearsal. "Candice Bergen," she repeated with an unbelieving sigh.

"Where?" Mike asked, coming up to them.

"We just missed her."

"I ran into Phil Donahue in the men's room," Mike informed them.

Alison and Jamie giggled.

"So my first star sighting was in the men's room. It's better than nothing."

"I thought we would see other stars around," Alison said. "This is billed as a star-studded cast."

Jamie knew the answer to that. "Not everyone comes to

rehearsal at the same time. The only people here now are the ones who'll be on during our half-hour block.''

Rodney, who had been running around the studio looking at the equipment, a special interest of his, headed their way. ''The assistant director says we're going to practice now. He wants us onstage in about five minutes.''

''But we haven't even been given any lines,'' a confused Alison said.

''Maybe they have cue cards,'' Mike suggested.

They walked out to the main stage, where the sound of hammering and sawing was drowning out the orchestra tuning up.

The harried assistant director gave them quick instructions. ''Mike and Alison, you come out stage left. Rodney and Jamie, stage right. Meet at the podium and read the lines on these cards. He quickly shoved some note cards into their hands and disappeared.

The kids looked at each other in surprise.

''I guess we'd better do it,'' Mike said with a shrug.

It wasn't much of a rehearsal. They did it twice, walking out, and then reading the lame jokes on the cards. When they finished, the same young man reappeared and said, ''Thank you very much. Be back here at six.''

''That's it?'' Alison said.

''I could have come up with better jokes than that,'' Rodney muttered.

Mike laughed. ''You're probably right.''

''Let's go home,'' Jamie said. ''And hope it goes better tonight.''

When they returned in the evening, it was a completely

different experience. Now, the glamour of the evening was in full force.

"Look over here. This way please," shouted a gauntlet of reporters and photographers.

Since Alison, Jamie, Mike, and Rodney appeared at the beginning of the show, they were immediately ushered backstage.

"Wow," Mike said, when they finally arrived. "What do they do with all those pictures?"

"Expect to see yourself in the tabloids," Jamie informed him. "Enquiring minds want to look at you all dressed up."

"I didn't know there were that many photographers in the world." Alison commented.

"I'm glad we look so good," Jamie said fervently.

Cindy had decided the girls needed new dresses after all, so they had spent the morning in their suite, trying on dresses that Cindy had chosen the day before from several department stores.

"What a way to shop," Jamie had commented.

"The stores don't mind," Cindy told her. "It will be a feather in their cap if you wear one of their outfits."

Alison had finally decided on a sea-green chiffon, full and flowing like something royalty might wear. She wore her hair loose and flowing.

Jamie was in slinky gold lamé. Her hair was in her signature French braid, but golden thread was woven through it for the occasion. The boys, of course, were wearing tuxedos.

"Julia Roberts was right behind us when we were com-

ing in,'' Rodney informed them. ''Maybe the photographers were really trying to get a picture of her.''

Jamie whacked him with her program.

They could hear the opening strains of the show's theme.
''How are you doing?'' Jamie asked Alison as the host
went into his opening monologue.

''I'm fine.'' She really was. Her success the day before
had settled her down. Besides, this seemed closer to doing
Sticks and Stones than doing a talk show. There were set
lines. She just had to forget that the audience consisted of
all the movers and shakers in the entertainment industry.
And of course block out the millions of viewers at home.

Jamie watched Alison calmly waiting to go on and wondered if her co-star had even an inkling of how close she
had come to not being there at all. Probably not. But that
was all right. Jamie had to admit that she felt pretty good
about her role in Alison's transformation. After the show
yesterday, Cindy had asked her for a moment alone. She
said Jamie and Mike and Rodney had performed a miracle
and that Alison was a go for the American Choice Awards.

Jamie hadn't felt even a pang of regret. Maybe, just
maybe, this was the beginning of a new relationship for her
and Alison.

Their stint on the awards show was over almost before
they knew it. They came out, read their little jokes—which,
surprisingly, the audience laughed at—and presented the
award for Favorite Children's Show. When a gaggle of
people came up to accept the award, the kids faded into the
background, then followed the winners out of the spotlight.
In just a matter of moments they were backstage. During a

commercial break, they would be seated in the audience, where they could enjoy the rest of the show in peace.

"I'm glad we were on at the beginning," Alison whispered when she was settled in her seat next to Mike.

"Me, too."

They watched several well-known celebrities give and receive awards.

"Does it ever surprise you that we're part of all this?" Alison asked.

Mike nodded. "All the time."

Alison knew that she'd be coming home to an empty house and had tried to steel herself for it, but it would have been great to have her parents waiting for her, to tell her how terrific she looked on television.

Not that she had been greeted entirely with silence. Estelle was excited enough for the whole neighborhood when Alison arrived home.

Alison hadn't even put her bags down in the front hall, when Estelle came flying out of the kitchen.

"Oh, Alison, you were wonderful! You looked beautiful! I feel like I should ask for your autograph."

"Don't be silly," Alison said, giving her a little hug.

Estelle fixed a cup of tea and demanded to hear every detail of the trip. It took a while, especially since phone calls kept interrupting.

Alison's grandmother was the first to phone.

"I taped you on the awards show," her grandmother said proudly.

"I thought you didn't know how to use your VCR."

"I paid the boy next door two dollars to set it for me. But he didn't get up early enough to get the *Today* show."

Even after her past success, Alison still burned with humiliation at the thought of her performance that day. "But you saw it live, right?"

"I did. I thought the other girl talked too much," her grandmother said indignantly.

Alison laughed out loud, to her grandmother's bewilderment. Trust her sweet old gran to blame all of Alison's shortcomings on Jamie.

Other friends and relatives who called tactfully avoided the topic of the *Today* show, focusing only on the American Choice Awards. Only Dana was bold enough to mention it.

"What was wrong with you on *Today*?" she asked bluntly. "Were you sick or something?"

"No. I was just nervous."

"You looked like you were going to pass out."

Great, Alison thought. That was a piece of information she could have done without.

"But you did fine on the awards show. Did you see any stars?" Dana demanded.

Alison was glad to get the conversation into safer waters. She plopped down on her bed, ready to fill Dana in on the whole glamorous evening.

After hanging up with Dana, Alison, so exhausted from her trip, was looking forward to a nice quiet evening at home. She threw on her oldest jeans and a torn T-shirt and put her hair up in a ponytail. No matter how much fun it was to get dressed up, it felt awfully good to get into some grubby clothes and relax.

Estelle stuck her head into Alison's bedroom. "What can I fix you for dinner?"

Rich food was another thing that Alison was tired of. "Oh, thanks, but I've been eating all week. I'll fix myself a grilled cheese sandwich."

"That's it?" Estelle asked with disappointment.

"Why don't you take the night off?" Alison suggested. "After I eat, I'm just going to hit the hay early."

"Well, if you think so . . ."

"I do." Alison smiled at her. "You can start taking care of me tomorrow."

Alison was pleased to have the house to herself. She decided to watch a little TV and then read the many cards and letters her parents had sent her from their various ports of call.

She had just settled in with a stack of mail when the doorbell rang.

"Now, who's that?" Alison wondered, getting up. She opened up the door to Mike.

"Oh no," Alison moaned.

"That's a nice greeting," Mike said with a grin.

Alison looked down at her outfit with dismay. "I look like a ragamuffin."

Mike shrugged. "I saw you last night and you looked like a vision."

"Thank you," Alison said quietly.

"Can I come in?"

"Sure," Alison opened the door widely. "Are you hungry?"

"Actually, I am. Is Estelle whipping something up?"

Alison shook her head. "Estelle's off. I'm the cook this evening. How do you feel about grilled cheese sandwiches?"

Mike pretended to think about that for a minute. "I am used to rack of lamb, but what the heck. I'll try your grilled cheese sandwiches."

"Gee, thanks so much."

"And maybe I'll make my special chocolate pudding for desert," Mike told her grandly.

"Sounds like a feast fit for a king."

"And queen," Mike added.

They walked into the spacious kitchen. Mike looked around. "It must have been something to grow up in a house like this."

Alison got out the bread, cheese, and butter. "Now you sound like Jamie."

Hoisting himself onto the counter, Mike said, "I know that Jamie's given you a rough time. Hey, no one was more suspicious of her than me. But I've got to hand it to her. She really came through for you."

Alison walked over and stood in front of him. "So did you."

"No. You came through for yourself." He pulled her to him and kissed her on the top of her head. "Now, how about those grilled cheese sandwiches?"

Jamie poured herself another diet cola. "Mom, I think I've told you everything. Twice."

"I know, I know. But there might have been some little

detail you missed. Some star you forgot to mention you saw?''

"I don't think so.'' It had been fun sharing all the excitement of the trip with her mother, but Jamie was still worn out. Ever since she had arrived home in the early afternoon, her mother had been following her around, eager for every detail. Even Elsie, who seemed to take it for granted that her sister was on a television show, seemed impressed by Jamie's appearance on the American Choice Awards.

"You were all dressed up,'' she told Jamie solemnly.

"Yes, I was.''

"You looked pretty.''

"Thank you.''

"Why don't we play dress up now?'' Elsie pleaded. "You can wear a pretty dress, and I'll put on the dress you were wearing on television.''

Jamie threw back her head and laughed. "Oh, so that's your idea, is it, pumpkin?''

Elsie looked a little confused. "Yes. Don't you think that would be fun, Jamie?''

"It would be fun, but I don't have the dress anymore. It was only borrowed.''

Elsie's face fell.

"Tell you what,'' Jamie said, pulling Elsie onto her lap. "Someday soon we'll play dress up. I do have a few new things you might like to try on.''

"Okay,'' Elsie said, happy once more. "Jamie?''

"What now?''

"I see your friend in the park?''

"What friend?'' Jamie asked.

"That boy."

"Oh, David."

Jamie had to admit that she had been thinking about David while she was gone. She didn't know why she should have wasted a moment on him, but at night, before she fell asleep, and when she woke up, David was always there.

Mrs. O'Leary got up from the kitchen table. "Are you hungry?"

Jamie shrugged. "I guess." She was still on New York time, and what she really was, was tired.

There was a knock at the door.

"I'll get it," Elsie cried.

"Ask first," Mrs. O'Leary cautioned.

"Who is it?" Elsie practically yelled.

"David."

Elsie looked at Jamie, who nodded to let him in.

"Hello," David said, coming into the kitchen.

"I didn't think I'd see you again," Jamie said icily.

Mrs. O'Leary sized up the situation. "Elsie, why don't we go to the park?"

Elsie looked curiously from Jamie to David. "I went to the park already."

"Then let's go to the library."

"Okay," Elsie said agreeably.

"Is that all right, Jamie?" her mother asked.

"Sure." She hoped her shrug made it clear that handling David was no problem.

"So," Jamie repeated, as the door closed, "I didn't think I'd be seeing you again."

"I acted like a jerk," David said, taking Mrs. O'Leary's seat at the table."

"You certainly did," Jamie agreed.

"It's just that being on television, well, you can't compare that to . . ."

"I know—*acting.*" Jamie's fake British accent said it all.

"Right," David said, subdued.

"David, what are you doing here? Slumming?"

"No. I saw you on the American Choice Awards."

"Don't tell me you were actually watching television. What happened? Did your cat turn it on by mistake?"

David ignored the sarcasm. "You looked wonderful."

"Well, thank you."

"I think we got off on the wrong foot, Jamie."

"That will happen when someone tells you you've picked a career for morons."

"I can see I made a mistake coming over here," David said, getting up. "I won't bother you anymore."

Jamie knew she should just let him walk out. Who cared if he left? Why, she hardly knew the guy. Instead, she jumped up and caught his arm. "Don't go."

"Why not?" David demanded.

"Because I don't want you to," Jamie said simply.

David considered this. "I guess that's a pretty good reason," he said with a smile.

Jamie led him over to the couch. "I could use your help tonight, David."

"What do you want me to do?"

She held up a thick binder that she had thrown on the

coffee table. "I need someone to run my lines for me. You know, for my television show?"

"Go over a television script with you?" David laughed. "I can't think of a better way to spend an evening."